HER DIRTY MAFIA

A MEN AT WORK REVERSE HAREM ROMANCE

MIKA LANE

HEADLANDS PUBLISHING

COPYRIGHT

Copyright© 2021 by Mika Lane
Headlands Publishing
4200 Park Blvd. #244
Oakland, CA 94602

ANNABEL "BEL" SIMMONS

"You're hired."

Wait?

What?

Hired? I'm *hired?*

Mr. Domenico Bonetti of BCL Enterprises, whose dark gaze drilled me so intensely that I had to wipe a dab of sweat from my temple, had just offered me a job.

This was the same man I'd only just met, and spoken with for ten minutes.

Actually, not even ten minutes.

And to be honest, I wouldn't even say he'd exactly *offered* me the job. He just told me I was *hired,* like it was a foregone conclusion I'd show up there the next day at nine a.m., coffee in hand, hoping I didn't have a run in my panty hose.

"Excuse me, Mr. Bonetti?"

I was sure I'd misheard. No one got a job this way.

Unless that was how they did things in Las Vegas. I mean, it *was* a pretty strange place.

My presumptive new boss, Mr. Bonetti, was likely called Mr. Hottie behind his back by his female employees. I knew the type. Devastatingly handsome. Women at his feet. He might wear blue jeans to the office to show he was a 'cool' guy, but he topped them with custom cut dress shirts with monogrammed cuffs barely hiding an obscenely expensive watch.

I'd bet money he got his hair trimmed at one of those fancy hipster barbers who charge guys a hundred dollars plus for a fifteen-minute trim.

I checked out his nails, expecting to see the clichéd man manicure.

They were perfect. Of course.

It wasn't like I was some sort of expert on men. I came from a podunk town in West Virginia where most of the men didn't even trim their nose hair.

But Len did. When we'd first met, I'd thought he was one in a million. A smart, funny guy who'd just blown into town, capturing the attention of every female for miles. He was well-groomed and well-dressed—by West Virginia standards, anyway—and swept me off my feet.

For some reason, out of all the women in town, he

zeroed in on me. And I ate it up. In all my twenty-six years, I'd never had someone pursue me like he did. Actually, I'd not really had anyone pursue me at all.

Sure, I'd had the infrequent date to play darts at the local bar, and the occasional attempt at casual sex, but nothing ever held my interest for long. I had my sights set on getting the hell out of town at my first opportunity.

And Len wanted to come with me.

What a shitshow that turned out to be.

Mr. Bonetti cleared his throat to get my attention. "Miss Simmons, I just said you're hired. For the PA job."

Okay. I *had* heard him right.

I knew that 'PA' meant *personal assistant*, thanks to good old Google. But what I didn't know, and what I planned to keep from Mister Hottie, was that I had no idea what a PA *was*. Or what a PA *did*.

When I'd arrived for my interview-that-was-not-an-interview, an impossibly sexy receptionist in a tight dress showed me to Mr. Bonetti's office. That is, after she'd looked me up and down with a sneer.

Thanks, lady.

Mr. Bonetti and his partners ran a hotel and casino and some other businesses I supposed I'd hear about at some point. Their offices were reached from the side of the hotel via a separate entrance from where the guests came and went. But the huge glass window behind him overlooked the hotel atrium. Good way to keep an eye on things.

And because his office sprawled the width of the building, the windows on the other side looked across Vegas to the mountains, as far as the eye could see.

There was so much to look at, I didn't see how he got anything done.

He sat behind a massive glass and chrome desk with oversized computer screens on either side, of course, because that's what guys like him did, right?

Cliché number two.

The middle of his desk was empty, save for a few papers and things, so he could see between the two monitors to the person sitting opposite. In this case, that was *me*. So friendly.

I'd taken the seat the receptionist had pointed to before she'd floated from the room, sinking my ass so far into some modern creation I didn't know how I'd get back out of it.

"Cool chair," I said, to cover my clumsiness.

"It's an Eames. An original."

Did everyone know what an *Eames* was, because I didn't.

But I smiled and nodded like I did.

"So Miss Simmons, what brings you to Vegas?"

I was dreading this question. It wasn't like I could tell him that I'd come to get away from a creep boyfriend, who'd found me here anyway. Or that I should have just stayed in my shitty small town because what was the point in running away if what you're running away from just follows you?

I smiled brightly. "I wanted something new. A fresh start."

Now *I* was a cliché.

And naturally, he looked at me like I was full of shit. But he was polite enough to cover it. "Yes. I can relate. Sometimes you just need... a new point of view."

We were connecting. Cool.

The interview, such as it was, continued like that—vague questions from him and vague answers from me—until he'd wrapped things up by telling me I had the job.

I was too embarrassed to admit I didn't even know what the job was. But a job was a job, and I needed one. Badly.

He knew nothing about my employment history. Didn't seem to care. Which was a good thing. If he had, he'd never have hired me.

That's how it goes when you have a police record.

Yup, I had a police record.

I'd stolen from my previous employer, a hardware store owned by the family I'd grown up next door to.

We'd been neighbors and friends. Until I stole from them.

Len had needed a seventy-dollar drill to fix the front steps of the house my sister and I had inherited from our aunt. Naturally, we didn't have seventy extra dollars for it. But Len had a solution. Just bring one home.

Take it. Nothing will happen.

Um, yeah. Thanks.

I felt like shit stealing from some of the nicest people I'd ever known and even as I stuffed it into my backpack, I vowed to find a way to pay them back. It was a terrible thing I did, but I told myself it was really just a loan against future paychecks.

I might even bring it back when we were done with it.

I made my move at closing time. There were no cameras or other security in the back of the store. I thought I was in the clear. But as luck would have it, I got just outside the door when the manager and his son grabbed me and pulled me back inside. They not only fired my ass, but they also called the police.

Our steps never got fixed.

But mister good-looking behind his big, Las Vegas desk didn't seem to give a crap about what I may or may not have done that day. Or any other day of my life. Thank god.

The shame of stealing from them was overwhelming, and I can guess the owners didn't feel too great about the way I'd betrayed them. They'd given me an opportunity that I'd thrown back in their faces.

A week later, when they'd dropped the charges, I bought a bus ticket to Vegas. I got a ride to the station while Len was out of the house and called my sister, who was off at college.

I didn't need a boyfriend who sat around the house and asked me to steal shit he couldn't afford.

But that wasn't the end of my dumb mistakes.

I'd told a girlfriend where I'd landed in Vegas. Len followed me by a few days, having driven his old Toyota.

He told me he had plans. He was going to make it big, playing poker.

He played a lot with his buddies and among them, he was usually the winner.

But a small town poker player does not a Vegas winner make. He borrowed against his credit card for the cash to get started.

And lost it just as fast.

2

ANNABEL "BEL" SIMMONS

WHEN I'D ARRIVED in Vegas and was directed to one of the cheaper motels in town—I didn't opt for *absolute* cheapest because who the hell knew what kind of people a place like that attracted?—I met a nice woman working the front desk.

"Where you from?" she'd asked, handing me my room key.

"West Virginia."

"Oh, wow. Clear across the country. Welcome to Las Vegas. I'm Kate." She extended her hand.

She was a big woman, tall and beefy. Long blonde hair fell down her back in a skinny braid, which kept falling forward over her shoulder as she bent to gather things for me—an entry card to the breakfast room, some paper brochures on Vegas helicopter rides, and a key to the swimming pool out front.

"It's just you, right? You're alone?" she asked, looking past me.

I followed her gaze out the lobby doors and into the parking lot filled with beat-up vehicles. I didn't see anybody. "What do you mean?"

"You'll be the only one in the room, right?" She laughed.

"Oh. Yeah. Nobody but me."

Then I got an idea. "Kate, do you know where I might find a job?"

She laid her hands on the counter between us. Her nails were bitten to the quick. "Well, we need a cleaning woman here. Ours just up and quit."

She caught me wrinkling my nose. "Okay, well, they need a clerk over at the mini-mart. I think it's a third shift sort of thing. You'd start at like eleven p.m. and go till six or seven a.m."

This time I controlled my face. What the hell had I expected, blowing into town, not knowing a soul? It's not like Vegas had been waiting for me with open arms, holding open some sort of cush job for the likes of me—an accused shoplifter.

I say accused because while the charges were dropped, I still had a record.

Mr. Bonetti stood. "Thanks for coming by, Miss Simmons. We'll see you tomorrow, then?"

I refocused. "Yes. Of… course. I'm… thrilled. Thank you, Mr. Bonetti."

As the receptionist led me back out, I scanned the office to see what I could learn about the place.

It was clear I was going to need new clothes. The women in the office—and there were quite a few of them—were pretty much routinely wearing snug, form-fitting sheath dresses, the kind I'd seen the women on *Real Housewives* wear.

I glanced down at my own outfit. No wonder the snotty receptionist had turned her nose up. The white blouse, black pants, and mismatched jacket I wore, which I'd picked up at Target on sale, begged for an upgrade. But I wouldn't see a paycheck for two or three weeks.

Guess the people I worked with were going to have to get used to me wearing my one black suit.

I could have avoided dress codes entirely by pursuing the mini-mart job, where I could have worn sneakers and jeans everyday.

But this opportunity, the one with Mr. Bonetti, was light years superior to the mini-mart. In fact, it was light years better than probably anything else in the world that I would ever land in my entire life.

And I had no idea why Mr. Bonetti had given it to me.

On top of everything, I was to be paid more money than I'd ever made. In fact, it was probably more than what my parents made together, back when they were alive. And certainly more than what my elderly aunt, who'd raised my sister and me after my parents died, got from her retired teacher salary.

I didn't even know what I'd do with all the money I'd be making. I mean, I was going to be far from rich, but for the first time in my life, I'd have enough money to cover my bills and best of all, help my sister pay for school. I'd even be able to eat in restaurants once in a while.

It might not be much to someone else, but to me it was everything.

"HEY, SWEETIE, HOW'D THE INTERVIEW GO?" KATE ASKED when I popped into the motel office after the interview.

I shook my head, still in disbelief. "They gave me the job. I'm hired."

Speaking the words out loud made me realize the good fortune that had just fallen into my lap. I closed my eyes, jumped up and down, and even squealed.

"Oh my god, girl, congrats," she said, beaming.

I rifled through my purse. "Before I forget." I handed her a little flip phone, which she'd loaned me 'just in case.'

She'd been good to me since the day I arrived.

"And thank you so much for letting me use the computer. I hope you don't get in trouble or anything."

She waved her hand. "No one will ever know."

When I got my first paycheck, first thing I'd do was take her to a nice dinner.

It had been Kate's suggestion that I look on Craigslist for work. I'd emailed probably twenty job listings, and Mr. Bonetti was the first to call me. Actually, he was the only one to call.

And one day later, I had a job. A fucking job. In an office. With people who dressed nice and said *please* and *thank you.*

When I'd responded to the ad, I told Kate I wasn't sure what a PA was. She didn't know either. A Google search indicated it was kind of like a regular admin job with a touch of errand running thrown in. The biggest takeaway was that it was pretty much whatever the boss wanted it to be.

Fine by me.

But I'd been sure they'd never call someone like me in for an interview, anyway, so why even bother applying? But Kate had said to go for it. What was the worst that could happen? I wouldn't hear from them and would try for a job somewhere else.

Their loss, as she said.

Oh shit. One more thing to do. "Hey, before I return the phone, can I call my sister really quick?"

She waved me out the door. "Go for it."

I stepped outside and dialed Maggie.

Sis!" she said on the first ring.

"Guess what," I said humming with excitement, "I got a job."

Maggie screamed over the phone. "Is it something good? Are you happy?"

I had to consider that for a moment. "I think it's good. And I think I'm excited. And I should have enough money to send you some for school."

I heard her voice catch from across the long distance. "No, Bel. I can't let you do that."

I waved my free hand even though she couldn't see me. "I can and I will. No arguments. Maybe you can drop one of your jobs to have more time to focus on school."

Now the wheels were turning. "Thank you. Thank you, Bel. Can you believe I have only two semesters left? My degree is almost within reach. As soon as I get my own job and start making money, I'll pay for you to go to college. Just hang on a little longer, okay?"

My heart broke at her earnestness. "Of course, Maggie. We're both doing our best."

Which was not too bad, all things considered. Our parents had died in a car crash when we were young, and an elderly aunt reluctantly took us in because there simply wasn't anybody else. In spite of her misgivings, she'd provided us a warm and loving, if austere home.

"Hey, before you go, I hear from the folks at home that Len hasn't been around town. He disappeared shortly after you left. Watch out in case he comes to Vegas."

It was a little late for that.

I didn't have the heart to tell her that not only had he come to Vegas, but he'd also promptly found me and was at that very moment probably sleeping in my motel room. Maggie had never liked him, and when I got busted for trying to steal the drill, well, that was the final nail in the coffin. I couldn't let her know that my efforts to start a new life were sullied by that jerk. We needed her focused on school.

"No way would he come here." I lied right through my teeth.

She gave a small laugh. "You're right. How would he ever find you? No one knows where you are. Except Sasha and me."

Exactly. Sasha, my big-mouthed former best friend who'd spilled the beans on my whereabouts. So much for discretion.

After our goodbyes, I returned the phone to Kate. "I don't know how to thank you."

She shrugged. "Glad to help someone move up in the world. Now, if I could only figure out a way to do it for myself."

She laughed, but behind it there was a sadness in her eyes. A pang hit my heart as it occurred to me that once I started making money and could leave the motel, chances were I'd no longer see much of Kate. We'd have the best intentions around getting together. Maybe we would once or twice. But as time passed, such outings would surely dwindle and then outright stop. I wondered if she were thinking the same.

She was no dummy.

"You're moving on to bigger and better things. I know it."

I swallowed the lump in my throat. "We'll keep in touch, Kate. I know we will," I lied.

I SLIPPED THE CARD KEY IN MY DOOR AND OPENED IT AS quietly as possible. If Len was sleeping, I wanted him to stay that way as long as possible. The more he slept, the less I had to deal with him.

But he wasn't sleeping. Unfortunately.

"Did you get the job?" he barked.

Shit.

"Yes. Got it."

I was suddenly tired. So tired.

"Hey, what did I tell you about your hair?"

I lifted my hand to find that most of it had fallen out of the bobby pins I'd secured it with before I left for my interview. In all the excitement, I hadn't noticed.

And why would I? Who cares if my hair is falling out of its bun?

Len cared. A lot.

"You need to keep your hair together. Why do I have to keep telling you that?"

Because I don't give a shit what you think...

I sighed. I was biding my time. Soon enough, I'd be rid of both him and the motel.

Until then, I was playing along.

He sat up straighter on the bed, where he spent most of his time, either sleeping or watching TV. "So how much they paying you?"

I decided to lie. Again. "A little over minimum wage."

He slammed his hand down on the flimsy motel nightstand. "Goddammit. Is that all?"

I nodded, pretending to be forlorn.

Instead, I was thinking about how my life was going to improve tenfold.

"Well, as soon as you get paid, I can get back to the tables. I'm gonna win big, Bel. I can feel it." He pounded his chest to make his point.

"Len, why don't you get a job?"

I was pushing it. I knew that. But a girl could take only so much.

Jumping to his feet, he stormed toward me. But I stood my ground, even when he was so close his cigarette breath made my eyes burn.

"Why?" he snapped. "So you can get rid of me? Like you did at home? Don't even try it. I will find you. I will always find you."

I darted for the bathroom and slammed the door while Len screamed on the other side of it. I turned on the tub faucet full blast to drown him out, and poured a little of the body wash my sister had given me into it for bubbles. I sank into the steaming water and closed my eyes. He finally shut up.

He thought I couldn't get away from him, but he didn't know shit. I was going to save every spare penny I could and move someplace secure, where he couldn't get to me. I'd work for that handsome Mr. Bonetti, the one who'd hired me for no good reason, and do such a great job for him, he'd wonder how he ever got by without me. Maybe he'd even give me a raise.

I'd never gotten a raise.

But then, I'd never gotten a job without a real interview.

3

DOMENICO "DOM" BONETTI

I HADN'T SEEN that one coming.

Miss Annabel Simmons, also known as 'Bel,' had thrown my morning off in a way that hadn't happened in a long time.

In a good way.

She was different. And sometimes different was good.

Unlike other women I usually interviewed for the company, Bel was not well-dressed. Her trousers were at least a size too big, and the sleeves on her unmatched jacket were too short for her lanky figure. Her flat shoes, more suitable for jeans than business wear, were scuffed to the point where there was little color left on the toes.

Nor was her makeup tastefully done. She struck me as one of those tomboyish women who wore makeup on special occasions, limiting their day-to-day routine to lip balm. Because of that, her unskilled efforts left her with unnaturally pink cheeks and smudges of mascara under her eyes.

And in spite of it, she was perfect.

The bitchy receptionist who'd shown her in—our fifth in as many months—had looked her up and down with a sneer before dropping her off in my office, swanning away with a little extra derrière shake for my benefit.

If she thought I'd fuck her, she was out of her mind.

I didn't do bitches, and I didn't do fake tits.

But Bel's natural style, aside from her effort to spruce herself up, was quite the contrast.

Her fiery red hair, shot with gold by the sun glaring through my office window, was pulled into a messy confection at the nape of her neck. In spite of her efforts to restrain it, misbehaving curls floated around her face like a halo. She was a bit on the skinny side for my taste, but I wasn't looking for a goddamn wife. And when she spoke, her large blue eyes locked with mine in a confident, if not defiant gaze, indicating a toughness I didn't see in women who came from more privileged worlds.

She reminded me of myself.

I couldn't lie. I was intrigued.

My weaknesses had gotten me into trouble before. They probably always would. Some men learned from their mistakes.

I didn't give a shit.

I was picky about my personal assistants. I had to trust them with every aspect of my life. I didn't give that sort of trust easily. The last good assistant I had moved to the Caribbean after being with me five years.

Yeah, I paid that well. If a PA stuck around and was loyal, they benefitted from the largesse of what I called my 'bonus plan'—an exponentially growing series of deposits made to a numbered offshore bank account.

When people took care of me, I took *very* good care of them.

My old assistant had come in off the street much the same way Bel had—new to Vegas, tired, hungry, and desperate for a break. She left with enough cash to never have to work again.

People like her who are otherwise out of good options make the best employees. Their loyalty and dedication are unmatched. Generally.

There's always the outlier who thinks they can pull a fast one. Those people don't stick around my office for long. In fact, they don't stick around Vegas for long. They're escorted out with an invitation to never return. An invitation they took very seriously once they fully understood the consequences of not complying.

Some might say I was taking advantage of the vulnerable, but that would be bullshit. I wasn't asking them for anything they wouldn't give another employer, including their trustworthiness. That was paramount.

And to those people? I could provide opportunities many people never get.

Like those I planned to provide Bel.

Granted, I couldn't stop thinking about that red hair and exacting gaze and how, with a few meals out in Vegas's top restaurants, she'd fill out nicely, turning some of her sharp corners into lovely curves.

I liked the way she drank in both my office and me, constantly assessing her surroundings and making mental notes on how to fit in.

If I knew anything about a person like her, after she got her first paycheck, she'd ask another woman in the office, one she'd become friendly with, having shared coffee or even a quick lunch, for shopping recommendations. She will have chosen this woman based on perceived kindness—Bel would be too smart to make herself vulnerable to any of the office bitches.

No, she wouldn't end up in a one-down position, at least not on purpose. She might not be an alpha girl, but I was pretty sure she wouldn't let one run her over, either.

She'd start to arrive at work in stylish new dresses, toned-down makeup, and tasteful manicures—perfect for a business setting. She'd look like she'd belonged here at BCL Enterprises since day one, and all memory of her shabby first appearance would be forgotten. Even by her.

What can I say? I know how to read people. I've had years of experience. And I suppose that's what's kept me alive.

"Hey, Dom. How was the PA interview?"

My associate Tristan, in his bespoke suit and gelled hair, helped himself to the very seat where Bel had sat just a couple hours earlier.

"Well, her name is Annabel Simmons. Goes by Bel. And I liked her."

Tristan's eyebrow rose. "Liked her? Or *liked* her?"

I didn't lie to Tristan, or to our other business partner, Sammy. "Both, actually," I said, avoiding his stare. I knew I was about to get some shit.

And right on schedule, he threw his hands up. "All right, Dom. She's hot. But there are hot women all over Vegas. I suggest you get your rocks off elsewhere. We're being careful about this sort of thing these days, remember."

He was right.

But what could I say?

I shrugged. I wasn't going to lose sleep over it. If Tristan wanted to, he was welcome to. "Sometimes these things just happen."

I was done discussing it. And I was fucking starving, making me grouchier than I already was. Another reason I needed an assistant ASAP. I hated going out for my own lunch—waiting in line, getting jostled, and carrying my shit back in a plastic bag. No, not for me.

And yeah, I could get delivery, but by the time it arrived, it always tasted like shit.

I looked out my office window. The view from our building's penthouse was staggering. You could see the entire Vegas Strip and the mountains beyond. The desert was an acquired taste they said, but I'd always thought it was beautiful.

"I hate Mondays," Tristan groaned, stretching in his seat.

Really?

"Tris, it's not Monday. Get your shit together."

He checked the date on his watch. "Oh. Right."

I tried to clear my mind of Bel. We had business to discuss. "So, what's up with the pawn shops, Tris?"

His face got serious. "Number three was held up two days ago, almost exactly a month after number one. They haven't hit two yet. I don't think they will because they know we have no jewelry or guns there."

It was the Russians. I was convinced of it. They were new to town, trying to gain a foothold, and needed cashflow. So they robbed easy targets—pawn-shops. Or what they thought were easy targets. They were about to learn they'd fucked with the wrong people.

My stomach knotted thinking about it, making me more pissed I was overdue to eat lunch. "When I get my hands on those fuckers—"

But Tristan interrupted me by holding up his hands. "Now, Dom, this is my baby. I'm taking the lead."

Whatever. I was pretty much done for the day anyway. I couldn't think straight since meeting Bel Simmons. Well, I *could* think—but only about her. Which was giving me an unfortunate semi-hard on, in spite of her needing a little more meat on her bones. Goddammit.

I nodded. "You're right, Tris. The pawnshops are your baby. Let me know how I can help."

Tristan knew more about our pawnshop business than either Sammy or me. He'd worked in them back in the day, first as a stocker-slash-janitor and then later as a clerk, when my dad was still in charge. He'd done such a bang-up job the old man put him in charge of all the stores and gave him a nice office in headquarters along with some sort of bonus.

The starry-eyed young Tristan went out and bought several suits and a new car, never looking back.

Now, the only time I ever saw him out of his custom-made clothing was when we went to the gym. He was a big believer in, as he put it, *looking his best.*

Sammy, on the other hand, dressed half the time like a roadie for a rock band. But it was all good. Business casual ruled the work world these days. And I liked to think I fell somewhere in between my partners, wearing blue jeans every day but topping them off with expensive as fuck dress shirts.

"So are you still going to hire that girl?"

I knew Tristan was going to think it odd I'd offered Bel a job without interviewing anybody else. Shit, I hadn't even checked her references.

I didn't want to. I couldn't give a shit what some former employer thought of her *workplace skills*.

I wanted her. And I wanted her now.

"She starts tomorrow, Tris."

4

DOMENICO "DOM" BONETTI

"Miss Simmons, welcome to BCL Enterprises."

With wide eyes, Bel looked up from her desk, where she would be taking care of my every whim from this day forward.

I was going to enjoy that immensely.

She was also wearing the exact same outfit she'd had on the day before, at her interview. Guess she hadn't had time to shop. Or more likely, didn't have the money to.

But I would help with that.

She stood, extending her hand. "Thank you, Mr. Bonetti. I'm so excited to be here. I'm going to work really hard for you."

While I appreciated her attempt at enthusiasm, I hated the fake bullshit everyone thought they were supposed to say on their first day at a new job.

She'd probably read some *Forbes* or *Wall Street Journal* article on how to survive your first day at a new job.

"I'm glad to hear that, Miss Simmons. I'll have the receptionist show you around this morning, get you set up with email and a computer, and then you and I will have lunch in my office. How's that sound?"

She blushed the lightest pink.

Jesus. If she kept that up, I'd be proposing to her.

And I was never getting married.

"Sounds great," she said cheerfully.

Was that cheerfulness real? Did she realize what an opportunity she had here at BCL Enterprises?

I think she did.

Because she'd probably had more than her share of life's shit sandwiches.

Take me, for example. My mother was a whore, and my father was a mob boss. I didn't know him, or much about him, until I was eighteen years old. That's when Mom came clean, revealing that he was not only alive, but also right here in Vegas. He'd just never wanted anything to do with me. So I found him, and convinced him to make up for all his years of neglect. That's how I ended up running his company. I artfully forced him out, and he ended up six-feet-under. thanks to stress and a heart attack. He took me in and I took him out.

Almost made up for all the shit my mother had gone through, including dying young of an undiagnosed illness. And hell, I got a career out of it.

Yeah, I used to be a bitter prick.

The bitchy receptionist who'd scoffed at Bel's appearance the day before—and whose name I still could not remember—had been given the task of showing our her around. She clearly wasn't happy about it. But that was okay. I didn't keep prima donna pains in the ass like her around for long, and wanted to torment her a little longer before I got someone to can her.

I never fired people. I left that to someone else.

There was a knock on my office door—not too loud, but not too soft. Bel stuck her head in.

I had no doubt she was nervous, and it was cute as hell that she was pushing herself to look assertive. I had to give her props for that.

I was quite sure she'd ever worked in an office. You'd think I'd know that much about her, since I'd hired her.

But I hadn't even asked.

"Mr. Bonetti, I have our lunch."

I pointed to a table in the corner of my office. "Thanks. You can set up over there, please."

She tucked a red curl behind her ear and slipped in. While our lunch was just take-out, she set the small table with cloth napkins and silverware.

Just as I was about to join her, my office door flew

open. I knew who it was before I even looked—there were only two people in the whole world who entered my office without asking.

"Dom, we need to talk to you about the new—"

But they stopped short when they saw I had a visitor.

Surprise washed over Sammy's face, and he raked his fingers through his mop of hair. "Oh. Excuse me. Didn't know you were in a meeting." He smoothed the wrinkles in his shirt. He never ironed.

If I remembered correctly, Sammy had a thing for redheads. I wouldn't be surprised if he sat down at the table and ate my lunch.

"Hey, we can come back, Dom," Tristan said, straightening his tie but also moving toward the door. He knew better than to cockblock me.

Sammy was still staring.

"We're just starting lunch, guys. But I'd like you both to meet my new PA, Bel Simmons. These gentlemen are the other letters in BCL Enterprises— Sammy Caputo, and Tristan Lastra."

"Welcome aboard, Miss Simmons," Sammy said, extending his hand.

Her face lit up in a brilliant smile. Damn her.

I was so screwed.

Actually, we all were.

"Please call me Bel." She shook their hands.

I took my seat at the table, dropping my napkin

onto my lap, signaling that I was starting lunch and that the guys could hit the road.

Maybe now Tristan understood why I'd hired Bel. Sammy sure as hell would get it.

"Um, sure thing, Dom. We'll catch up later. It was nice meeting you, Bel," he said.

They left, quietly closing the door.

They were probably going crazy at that very moment, wondering where the hell I'd found her, and what kind of future she might have with the company… and us.

Bel poured dressing over her Cobb salad and dug in.

Why did women always get Cobb salads? They were like the Golden Retrievers of takeout lunches. Safe, predictable, likable. Impossible to offend. Boring.

I dove into my chilled steak tartare on a bed of arugula.

Fucking amazing. Probably my favorite lunch ever. One of the things I loved about modern-day Las Vegas. The food was awesome and you could find anything you wanted pretty much twenty-four-seven.

"How long have you been here in Las Vegas, Mr. Bonetti?"

Ah, small talk. The bane of my existence.

She dabbed her mouth with a napkin, and I saw she'd nearly finished her salad. Jesus, she must have been starving.

"Bel, you can call me Dom."

She laughed and shimmied her shoulders. "Okay, *Dom*."

And my dick got harder.

"And as for Vegas, I grew up here. Inherited the business from my father."

She didn't need to know the gory details behind that.

She nodded politely. "That's nice."

"What about you? I know you're new to Vegas."

Her shoulders slumped for a moment and when she realized it, she perked back up. "Grew up in West Virginia. My sister and I were raised by an aunt after our parents died in a car wreck. She was a retired schoolteacher, my aunt, so things were… tight."

I looked at her for a moment before deciding to share more about myself. Oh, what the fuck. "We have a lot in common. I grew up… on the wrong side of opportunity myself."

Her eyebrows rose. "And look at you now."

Yeah. She got it.

"So you're after a new beginning. What does that look like?"

She pressed her lips together and looked across my office, out the window at the mountains. I pretty much knew what she was going to say, knowing what it was like to want to reinvent yourself. But I wanted to see if she'd thought through the specifics.

"I needed to come to a place with better job opportunities to help my sister pay for college. She works three jobs and has taken out all these loans. Then when she's done, she'll pay for me to go. If I want, that is."

And there it was. Everyone had a fucking story, and now I knew Bel's. Part of it, anyway.

She was scrappy like us guys, coming in here knowing she wasn't as glam as the other women around, and still managing to hold her head up anyway.

That got my motor revving. And it didn't hurt that she was stunningly beautiful.

It had gotten to be the time of day when the sun blaring through the windows heated my office like a greenhouse. The AC would kick in momentarily, but until it did, it would be sweltering for a few minutes.

"You know, Bel, you can take your jacket off. We try not to be too formal around here, and in the afternoon my office gets hot. The problem with western-facing windows."

She looked at my rolled-up shirtsleeves and shrugged despite the thin line of perspiration on her upper lip. "Oh. I'm fine. Thanks."

She jumped to her feet like she had somewhere to be. "Is there a kitchen where I can take these things?" she asked, piling dirty dishes and food onto a tray.

"Yup. Down the hall on the right."

"Thank you for lunch," she said, backing out of my office with her hands full.

I went back to my desk, cursing myself for having

chosen a western exposure, when I saw a fork that had fallen on the floor under the lunch table.

Since I was looking for a chance to procrastinate, I headed to the kitchen with it.

And what I saw put the next few weeks of my life on a different track.

In the kitchen, cleaning up our lunch dishes, Bel had slipped her jacket off.

And in doing so, had exposed several large, hand-print bruises on her arms.

5

———————

DOMENICO "DOM" BONETTI

"Hey, Dom. Just got your text. Did you want to talk about the shipment stuck in Long Beach?"

I did want to talk about that. Imports were one of our more profitable… businesses. Sure, we did well with the hotel, casino, restaurants, and pawnshops, but that's not where the big money came from.

Imports were where the *fuck you* money came from.

The kind of money even rich people only dreamt about.

But that conversation could wait.

I waved at Sammy to close my office door. "Right now I have something else on my mind, Sam. I need to talk to you about the new PA—"

"The hot one?" he interrupted. "With the red hair?"

I lowered my voice. The door might be closed but she was just on the other side of it. "Yes, the hot one with the red hair, Sammy. Listen, she took off her jacket today and her arms were covered in bruises."

Sammy looked at me in silence, then fell into a chair, staring at his hands. "Shit."

My sentiment exactly.

I felt for Bel. But were the kind of problems that came with bruises the kind of things the guys and I ought to take on?

Tristan had been right. I needed to stop thinking with my little head. Fucked me up every time.

"What are you going to do about it?"

Let her go. At least that's what I *should* do.

But I wouldn't.

"I want you to follow her home tonight. See where she lives. Find out what her situation is."

We shouldn't get involved kept playing in my head.

And I ignored it.

I continued. "There's something about her, Sammy. She has the fight in her. She's one of us. I know we should walk away. But I can't. We can't."

He sighed and looked up at the ceiling. "I get your concern for her, but I don't know what you think we'll find that we don't already know. Bruised arms on a woman come from one place—an asshole husband or boyfriend."

He was right.

And yet.

"I know. But please do it."

He shrugged and got to his feet. "Sure. I'll let you know what I find out. And for what it's worth, I see the same spark in her that you do. It's a good call to see what she's up against."

Fucking A. I didn't know much about the woman. Hell, I didn't know anything about her thanks to my slack-ass interview.

And then I'd embarrassed the shit out of her, without thinking, by asking her about the bruises. She'd turned bright red and looked like she wanted to crawl away and hide. I'd only succeeded in humiliating her.

She didn't deserve that.

She'd pulled her jacket back on as if to say *conversation over*.

I'd seen women in situations like hers before and couldn't keep my mouth shut. I wouldn't keep my mouth shut, and neither would the guys. And while we engaged in some legally questionable activities in our business dealings, we didn't stand for someone taking his frustrations out on a woman. Shit like that didn't fly.

If I never saw Bel again after today, I'd still make sure that whoever had put those bruises on her arms would never do that again. It was just the way I was wired. All us guys were.

After she'd gone for the day, with Sammy on her

trail, I headed to the penthouse I shared with the guys. I needed some time alone.

Because we owned the best hotel and casino in Vegas, I could stop in any of the restaurants scattered through the hotel for something to eat or a drink anytime I wanted. And I did that a lot. I needed to get out and see things from the guests' perspective. Half our employees didn't even know who I was. Which was fine with me. It was the best way to assess our operations.

But tonight I needed to chill. I was uneasy with the day—first, having Bel join my team, then finding out she had some sort of shitty person in her life hurting her.

Things were never easy. Never.

My cell buzzed, sooner than I'd expected it to.

"Sammy? What'd you find?"

He muttered under his breath at the Vegas traffic. "She's at some shit motel on the other side of town. Close to where one of the pawn shops is."

Christ. That area left a lot to be desired. I *knew* she had a story.

"I didn't see much beyond that, Dom. She stopped by the office to talk to the front desk clerk and then headed up to her room."

Well, shit.

"No worries, Sam. This is a good start. There's a dude around there somewhere. She didn't put those bruises on herself."

"So what's the next step?"

I knew I could count on Sammy. I always could. Even if he didn't agree with whatever wild-assed plan I had up my sleeve, he'd support me in it.

"I'm going to get her out of there, plain and simple."

She didn't deserve to be living in a fleabag motel, wearing the same clothes every day, devouring her lunch because she was so goddamn hungry.

My reservations about having taken on an employee with some ugly baggage were waning. I could help make this woman's life better.

And I would.

6

ANNABEL "BEL" SIMMONS

"IS THIS MONEY FOR ME, Mr. Bonetti?"

Was I already getting the raise I'd fantasized about?

Nah. Not possible.

I hadn't done a thing for it aside from scheduling some meetings for Mr. Bonetti. Or rather, Dom. I'd hardly dazzled him with my top-notch skill of picking up a phone and dialing it.

Which made it even more strange that he was giving me a thousand dollar check when it was only my third day on the job.

His lips crooked into a little smile.

Yes, I'd been staring at his lips. It couldn't be helped.

And because I didn't know him well yet, I couldn't

tell if he was smirking, or if that was his 'resting polite face.'

"I know what it's like to be new in town." He spoke with a sureness that made my heart pound.

Which pissed me off. I did not need to be attracted to my new boss. I had enough problems.

But the way he looked at me… was thrilling. Like I was *somebody*. And not just somebody, but a somebody worthy of respect.

It also scared the shit out of me.

He continued. "When you're new in town, it can take a while to find your footing."

What the hell did that mean? Did he think I was a charity case? I glanced around the office. No, I wasn't dressed as nicely as the other women, but if someone had a problem with that, they could just—

I'd had a little money when I'd arrived in Vegas from the cash my sister and I had found in our aunt's house after she passed away, hidden in a shoebox in the back of her closet. We'd used a chunk of it for the cremation, and what remained, we split. Maggie was putting hers toward school, and I used mine to get out of town.

In addition to the cash, we'd inherited our aunt's rickety old clapboard house. We planned to sell it at some point, not that it was worth much, but while Maggie was in school, she needed a place to come home to. So any proceeds from that were on hold.

I needed to make my money last. There was no

other option. I'd had no idea how long it would take to get a job and get settled. Absolute necessities were the only things I was spending on. But wouldn't you know it, just as I was getting a feel for the place, Len showed up, like a bad dream.

At first, I thought maybe it was nice to see a friendly face. I'd been a little lonely. But it didn't take long to remember why I'd wanted to get away from him.

And it didn't take long for him to drain me of the little money I had.

"Bel, are you okay?"

My attention snapped back. "Yes. Sorry."

"I want you to take this, Bel. It's an advance on your salary. A lot of people need a little... boost when they're starting out."

I looked over the check. I didn't have a bank account yet. Another detail. You needed money to open a bank account, but you needed a bank account to cash a check.

Fucking banks.

"You can cash that downstairs in the casino if you need to."

Okay. He was a mind reader, too.

I still wasn't convinced his 'advance' was a sound idea. People didn't just give out checks for a thousand bucks, at least not where I came from. But shit, that money could come in handy while I waited for my first paycheck.

As soon as I pictured what I could do with one thousand bucks, alarm bells went off.

What was he going to expect in return?

Aside from my paying him back?

Yeah, no.

"This is very kind, Dom, but I can't accept it. And how do you know I'm good for it? How do you know I'm not going to just take off with your money and never come back to BCL Enterprises?"

The crook of his smile grew to a full-on grin.

So nice I could amuse him.

"Oh, you're good for it, Bel."

The power of that simple statement took my breath away. I casually put my hand on my desk to hide my attempt to steady myself.

I didn't know what it was about this man, but I smelled trouble.

Not necessarily bad trouble, like the kind where you're scared or feel hopeless. No, it was more like *fun* trouble, where something exciting lay around every corner.

And it seemed like I was accepting the money whether I wanted to or not. He was so matter of fact about it. "Thank you. I appreciate it. And I will pay you back. I don't need handouts Mr. Bon—I mean, Dom."

While I was praying he'd return to his office, desperate as I was to mop up the sweat between my boobs, he wasn't done. I was terrified I might start to smell since I hadn't been able to afford deodorant in a couple weeks.

Next, Dom reached into his front pocket and handed me a small flip phone.

"What's this?"

Everything I knew screamed that stuff like this didn't come without strings attached.

But still. I did need a phone.

He was amused. "Bel, I believe this is called a phone. Or a cell phone. You don't have one, do you?"

Was there anything this man didn't know about me? Shit, he could probably tell what color underwear I had on.

I shook my head. "I don't have one, you are right. Thank you."

I turned it over in my hand. It was tiny and light, just like the one Kate had loaned me for a couple days.

"It's what is called a burner phone. It will tide you over until you get some kind of smart phone. Give some thought to which one you might like."

Shit, was he getting me a smart phone too?

Maybe he could get me a house and car while he was at it.

The elevator dinged, diverting my attention. Dom's business partner Sammy burst through the doors and headed straight for us, hair flying.

He was good-looking but so different from Dom, with his dark, shoulder-length hair, worn blue jeans, and fitted but also wrinkled collared shirt.

He glanced at Dom, then settled his gaze on me.

I was done. Surely they could smell my B.O.

He put his hands on his hips, drawing attention to his perfectly flat stomach. He nodded at us. "Dom. Bel."

They looked at me like I was capable of saying something interesting. So, I did my best to prove them wrong.

"Hi, Sammy. Dom gave me a phone."

Oh my god…

He held his hand out for it. "Here. I'll put my number in it."

"Put mine in too. And Tristan's," Dom said.

I was going to have all three of their cell numbers?

"That's very nice. Thank you. But I don't imagine I'll be calling you much." I laughed breezily.

"You never know."

He returned my phone, and a dark tattoo peeked out from under his cuff.

I hadn't taken him for the tattoo type. He seemed so… office-y, in spite of his apparent preference for blue jeans and wrinkled shirts.

But when he ran his fingers through his mop of hair, his rock 'n roll side became obvious.

I could just see him in the front row of a stadium concert wearing a faded band T-shirt, scraping his hair back into a ponytail because he was dripping with sweat from pumping his arms in the air.

Focus.

He stole a glance at Dom. "It's our pleasure, Bel. Vegas isn't always safe for a woman… on her own."

Dom agreed, nodding. "It's true. A woman needs to protect herself."

Oh. Okay. I got it now.

This was a reaction to the bruises I'd stupidly let Dom see yesterday.

How fucking idiotic was I?

Len and I had gotten into it just a few nights before and he'd grabbed my arms during our argument. He was strong, and his grip hurt. But I never thought he'd be leaving imprints of his fingers.

As soon as he realized what he'd done, he began to cry and beg forgiveness.

And now it was clear that Dom had taken it upon himself to tell Sammy and probably Tristan, too. I couldn't blame him—they were business partners—but now they all knew how screwed up I was.

First money, then a phone.

Funny how guys took care of problems.

Sammy followed Dom into his office and closed the door.

I scrolled through my phone and looked at the three new numbers in it.

7

ANNABEL "BEL" SIMMONS

I WAS ASSAULTED BY LIGHTS, noise, and cigarette smoke when I ventured into the hotel's casino after work to look for a place to cash my check. It was funny. I was now working for the owners of a huge casino, and I'd never even spent any time in one. I mean, why would I? I didn't have money to throw around.

I didn't even have money for freaking deodorant.

And now that I was in one, I realized I hadn't been missing anything. The chaos was overwhelming in spite of the fact that there were barely any gamblers around since it was dinnertime.

Casinos drove even Len up a wall, at least that's what he always told me. He bragged how his poker games were held in fancy suites far above the gambling floor, as if he were some sort of elite casino patron.

Never mind that he'd lost all my money.

Spotting a row of what looked like bank tellers under a huge glowing sign that said *Cashier*, I headed over.

"Hi, honey. What can I do for ya?" a woman with bleached blonde hair asked me after she'd snapped her gum a couple times.

I pushed the check toward her.

She turned it over a couple times, her eyebrows raised. "Well, looky at this. A check from the big boss."

With a smirk, she looked me up and down, probably concluding I'd earned the money lying on my back.

"It's a cash advance. I'm Mr. Bonetti's new assistant."

She pressed her lips together in disgust. "Sure you are, honey. Now endorse the check so I can give you your money and you can be on your way. How do you want it?"

How many other BCL employees had come down here to cash checks from the 'big boss?'

"Um, I don't know. Hundreds and twenties, I guess?"

She reached into a drawer under the counter and came back with a stack of bills she counted in a blur.

"You want an envelope?"

"No. No thank you." I stuffed the wad of bills into

the bottom of my purse and headed straight to the grocery store.

Fifty dollars later, I pulled into the motel parking lot and hustled up to my room with all my purchases.

"Where the fuck have you been?" Len snapped, not looking away from his Jeopardy episode.

I set everything down on the one clean spot on the dresser, and Len screamed at the TV.

"How do these fucking losers get on this show? I could blow any of them out of the water any day of the week," he spat.

"Why don't you go on the show then?" I asked.

He finally looked my way. Which was not necessarily a good thing.

"*Why don't you go on the show?*" he mimicked.

I hated when he did that.

Actually, I hated pretty much everything he did.

He slammed his hand on the bed over a player's wrong answer. "I'm gonna try out for that show one day. You'll see. I'll make a fortune off those assholes."

When he lifted his head from the bed pillow, he spun his ball cap around so the bill was in the back— his favorite way to wear caps.

He gestured toward my packages with his chin. "What'd you get there? What's all that shit?"

I opened a beer and brought it to him.

"Is that where you've been all this time? *Shopping?*"

At this point, my only hope for peace was to keep feeding him beers until he passed out.

"Yeah, Len. I got us some food, too. You know, since I have a job now."

Crap. I'd left all my cash just floating around in my purse. I needed to hide it before he found it and demanded to know where I'd gotten it. And took it for himself.

I dropped my purse onto the floor next to the bed and kicked it out of sight. I wasn't keeping my money from him just for the hell of it. I needed to send some to Maggie, and if all went according to plan, in a couple weeks have enough cash left to get out of this motel and away from him.

That time was coming, and soon.

He finally got off the bed to inspect my purchases. Yanking a bag of chips open, he stuffed his mouth.

"Where'd you get the money for all this? I thought you said you wouldn't get paid for a couple weeks."

I shrugged lightly. "My boss gave me a little advance. Guess he could tell I needed it."

Len lowered his head and glared at me like a bull about to charge.

"You better not be lying to me."

When I'd first met Len, he'd been so put together. But when he started losing at poker, it was like he'd also lost his mind. Now, his dirty blond hair and scraggly goatee were beyond ugly, just like his personality.

"I'm not lying Len. Geez, would you relax?"

"Really? Then where the hell did you get THIS?" he

screamed, chucking the phone I'd made the mistake of taking out of my pocket.

I ducked too late and the phone, while light and small, was thrown with such velocity it bounced off my cheekbone, hit the wall, and shattered.

Wincing, I ran to gather the useless pieces of plastic. "Oh my god. Why did you do that? They gave me that at work."

He snatched the pieces of phone out of my hand. "You'd better not be whoring around. So help me—"

I sprinted to the door and yanked it open, running down the stairs to the Kate.

She looked up from the book she was reading. "Oh my god, honey, what happened?"

Taking my hand, she brought me over to the lobby's old sofa. "You're shaking. Did you get in a fight with Len?"

I took a deep breath, fighting tears. I wasn't going to let that creep make me cry.

"I got a phone at work and Len threw it against the wall. It's in pieces." I held out the one piece of plastic he'd not snatched from my hand.

"Well, shit. So much for that phone," she said, picking up the piece and turning it over in her fingers.

I brought my fingers to my cheek. First, bruises on my arm, then my face. Great way to make an impression at a new job.

"It hit me here before it hit the wall." I rubbed the spot that had already sprouted a little bump.

"You've got to get out of there, Bel," Kate said, examining my face.

"I know. I know. I'm trying. I got the job, now I just need to save a little money and find a new place. Which he'll probably follow me to, anyway."

I threw my hands up.

Kate disappeared behind the counter, returning with her purse. "No, he won't follow you. Not this time. You'll be someplace safe. Now here. Take this."

She handed me a tube of makeup. "You'll have a bruise tomorrow."

Fuck.

I could see it now. If I came into work with a bruise on my face, Dom would probably buy me a freaking handgun and teach me how to fire it.

Which might not be a half-bad idea.

And it finally occurred to me. The guys were protective. They barely knew me, but had assessed I was in a bad situation.

They weren't doing these nice things to get in my pants. They wanted to help.

I kept fighting the tears, but that didn't stop my voice from trembling. "I don't know what I'll tell them at work. They already know about the bruises on my arms. Now the phone is destroyed, and I have a bruise on my face."

They were going find my life was more fucked up than they even thought.

"Maybe I just won't go back."

That was one solution. Take the guys' money and run.

Yeah, right.

Kate sighed patiently. "Just tell them you dropped the phone. Phones break all the time. Everybody knows that. And tell them you bumped into a door to get that bruise on your face."

The cliché that was my life was becoming more pitiful.

But Kate was right. I had to lie. I had to keep that job.

Dom may or may not believe me about the phone, and may or may not believe me about my bruised cheek, but it really didn't matter as long as I could keep working there.

My goal was to make money to get my ass out of a bad situation.

I'd keep my eye on the ball, no matter how far out of reach it seemed.

8

SAMUELE "SAMMY" CAPUTO

"Good morning, Mr. Caputo."

I wished people didn't call me that. Every damn day, *good morning, Mr. Caputo* followed me from the elevator to my office. No matter how many times I told people to call me Sammy, some office manager for the company, who I didn't even know, kept telling our employees to address the guys and me with *mister*. I hated it.

Dom, on the other hand, relished it. Made him feel like a big shot. He was into that sort of shit. Hierarchy. Structure. Status.

I guess that was a comfort for him. I found it suffocating. I hated all kinds of rules. It's why I wore jeans and T-shirts to work most days. A wrinkled collar shirt if I felt like dressing up. Dom and Tristan didn't like it. They thought I should dress more 'professionally.' So, I compromised by occasionally wearing a nice English Laundry dress shirt. With my jeans. Sometimes I ironed it. Most times I didn't.

But it was all good. Our businesses were raving successes, and if acting like a partial grown up was the price I had to pay to get there, it wasn't an unreasonable one.

The calendar alert on my computer buzzed. I had five minutes until a meeting with the guys, so I headed for the stairwell.

Each of us had offices on different floors surrounded by the employees who made our businesses run—Dom was on the top floor surrounded by those who managed the hotel and casino. I was one floor below, where my team and I managed all food-related stuff—the hotel restaurants, bars, and catering. And Tristan was on the next floor down with the small team it took to run his pawnshop empire.

We also had other... associates, but they weren't in the BCL Enterprises tower. Those people, who helped with our more cash-intensive enterprises, were for the most part free agents. They came on board for jobs as we needed them. Like helping with the big shipment we were expecting, which had just arrived by ship in Long Beach, the west coast's largest port.

And the hotel was the perfect cover for it all.

We normally met in Dom's office. It was just a default kind of thing, a habit we'd fallen into, I guess because he'd taken over for his dad. In a sense, he was the head guy of our three-person team. But we owned the businesses equally. That way, no one could ever screw the other over if, god forbid, there was some sort of unsolvable conflict or disagreement.

I exited the stairwell and crossed the floor to Dom's office.

"Morning, Mr. Caputo."

Goddammit.

There sat Bel, Dom's beautiful redheaded assistant. I had a thing for redheads. And this was one of the prettiest ones I'd ever seen. Big blue eyes, full lips... I wondered if I could get her to take her hair out of that clip...

Focus.

"Bel, please call me Sammy. Seriously, it's okay."

"Okay. Sure." She smiled and went back to work. Whatever her work was. Dom always needed an assistant, but I never knew what they did.

I suspected not much.

But hey, he paid them out of his budget, so I didn't give a damn.

The elevator dinged and we turned to see Tristan running—it was now one minute past start time. He hustled past Bel and me so fast I could smell the soap he'd used in the shower.

He held the door to Dom's office open. "Coming?"

"In a minute."

He rolled his eyes and closed the door.

I looked back at Bel, who was either busy or really good at pretending to be, because at first, she didn't realize I was standing over her.

Dom had hired her because he was enchanted, not that he'd ever admit it. I couldn't blame him for it. She was fucking delicious by any measure. Doubted he'd get much work out of her, though.

I didn't think she'd ever worked in an office.

She finally looked up.

Well, *sort of* looked up. She was keeping one eye on her computer screen, which was odd because I knew she didn't have a hell of a lot to do.

So I moved directly into her line of sight, and immediately saw why she'd been trying to look away.

A familiar rage coursed through my veins.

Dammit.

She had a shiner on her cheekbone.

"Was there something I can help you with, Sammy?" she asked with a polite smile, still trying to turn the injured part of her face away from me.

She knew I'd seen her bruise in spite of the makeup trying to cover it. She began to blush, starting at the neck of her blouse, over her cheeks, and up to her forehead.

On top of everything else, she was now humiliated.

So I decided to let her off the hook.

"That hair of yours is incredible, Bel."

It was an overly familiar thing to say to an employee, but hell, it had been on my mind since the first time I'd met her.

From what I'd seen, she always kept her curls pinned neatly at the back of her neck in one of those messy knot-things that seemed so popular. Because it was early in the day, it was still tidy, with just a few hairs flying around her face. But in a few hours, she'd look like she'd just gotten out of bed.

And Christ if that didn't make my dick hard.

She reached for her hair at my compliment and smoothed it down, checking the security of the knot holding it together.

"Thank you."

I'd clearly embarrassed her again, but she needed to get comfortable with compliments. I was only too happy to help.

"Do you ever let it down? You know, take those pin things out?"

I was dying to pull them out myself, and feel that hair slip through my fingers...

Jesus. Get a grip, asshole.

Her mouth opened and closed while she chose her answer. "Um... yes. I wear it down. Sometimes. I just didn't think it was professional at work to do that. And my boyfriend, well, he doesn't like it loose—"

And there we had it. There *was* a dude in the picture. Which we pretty much already knew. How else would she be covered in bruises? And what was the asshole telling her about her hair?

But any talk of a boyfriend came to an abrupt stop. She'd clearly slipped, saying more than she'd planned to.

She stared up at me with those big eyes, like a kid who's afraid they're getting in trouble.

The guys were going to wonder what was taking me so fucking long. But I wasn't done with her.

"Take it down," I said quietly.

Her lips parted slightly and she stared at me for a moment. Then she reached behind her head and with a couple tugs, curls spilled down her back and over her shoulders.

Holy shit. She was like a renaissance painting.

"Stunning. You're stunning, Bel."

"Thank you," she whispered.

It was erotic as fuck, her gaze glued to mine the whole time.

"Um, Sammy. I have something to tell you." She cleared her throat and took a sip from the water bottle on her desk.

"What's that, Bel?"

I imagined her saying she wanted me to rip her clothes off and press her against the wall right then and there. Thank god I was holding a notebook because my boner was screaming for attention.

She looked around nervously. "The, um, phone you guys gave me. Well, it's gone. Broken. Destroyed."

The guilt in her eyes about killed me. I didn't give a shit about that stupid burner phone. We had boxes of them.

But I *was* interested in how the phone came to be destroyed, and whether it was somehow related to the bruise on her cheek.

"What happened?"

She reached into her purse and retrieved a plastic shard. "I dropped it. I'm so sorry."

Okay, we all drop our phones. But when we did, they didn't shatter into a hundred little pieces. And even though I was looking at a small remnant of what had once been her phone, it was pretty clear there was more to the story than what she was sharing. But we'd get into that later.

"Bel, don't worry about it. It was just a burner phone. They're cheap and we have tons of them. I'll get you another."

Her face brightened a little. "Really? Oh, thank you so much. I promise to be more careful this time. I'm just so… clumsy."

She laughed nervously.

Clumsy, yeah right.

9

SAMUELE "SAMMY" CAPUTO

THIS TIME, I followed Bel home without Dom suggesting it. I had a bad feeling about the bruise on her face. Dom hadn't mentioned it, but that wasn't a surprise—he'd had a crazy busy day and probably didn't even notice it—but I was haunted by it. Even when I went to jerk off in my private bathroom, thinking about her and her curly red hair. Turned out, I was so angry I couldn't even come.

And that made me even madder.

There was only one thing to do. Find out what she was up against, and remove her from the situation.

Pretty simple.

When we reached her motel, she stopped by the office like she had the night before. She spoke to the same woman, their heads bobbing up and down as they chatted.

While they talked, I gave Tristan a call.

"Sammy. What's up?" he answered.

"Tris. I'm at the Motel Vegas watching out for Bel. You're familiar with this part of town. What do you know about the place?"

"Dude, you're following her again?"

"Did you see the bruise on her face?"

Even saying the words made me want to puke, such a visceral reaction they caused me. This wasn't the first time I'd known a woman in this situation. I'd grown up with one.

My mother.

And I'd sworn on her grave I'd do whatever I could do to keep it from happening to anyone else.

"I did see it. What do you think is up?"

"I can only guess. I'm gonna find out."

He sighed deeply. He might not have the same reaction I did to this sort of thing, but he was no less committed to helping where he could. "The Motel Vegas, you said? Yeah, that's a shit part of town. I go by the place all the time. I see druggies come and go out of the parking lot and there are a lot of kids playing in the dirt. I take it that's where she's living?"

Bel headed for the door, and turned to wave at her friend.

"Tris, I gotta go."

"Do what you have to do. But be careful."

When Bel emerged from the motel office, the friendly, happy expression she'd worn slipped from her face.

I didn't like that.

Head down, she jogged up the stairs, hustling down the exterior corridor to her room. Before entering, she put her ear to the door. Then, she opened it slowly. Before it was fully closed, I could hear yelling all the way down in the parking lot with my car windows rolled up.

Jesus. It was worse than I thought.

Fuck this.

I got out of my car and headed for the stairs. Just when I reached the top, Bel's door flew open and she tried to run out. But before she could get away, she was yanked back into the room.

The door slammed shut.

From the other side of it came male shouts, and female crying. It transported me back to the days of my childhood when my mom had managed to say the wrong thing and bring on the wrath of my alcoholic father.

It was all so familiar.

And so was the rage building in my chest. When I was a kid, I couldn't do anything.

But I could now.

I pictured my mother as I kicked the door open,

wishing I could have done the same those many years ago.

And, like years ago, I came face to face with a familiar, ugly situation.

In two long steps I was across the room with a grip on the skinny upper arm of the loser who'd been causing Bel's problems.

"Let go of her before I break your neck."

He did, but continued to rant. "You fucking whore. I knew it. You have a brand new phone? Who'd you fuck to get another phone?"

He lunged for her, but with my grip on his arm, I swung him back into the wall behind us. He slammed into it and slithered to the floor in a daze.

Bel had her hand over her mouth, watching me with red eyes.

In the commotion, the phone that seemed at the core of the immediate problem had fallen to the floor. I grabbed it and handed it to Bel.

"Get your purse and wait downstairs for me."

She looked at the guy, then me, like she was making a decision.

But she had no decision to make, because I made it for her.

"Go," I shouted. "Go now."

I didn't know if she was more terrified by the boyfriend or my yelling, but she grabbed her shit and left.

Which meant it was time to deal with the loser.

Pulling him up off the floor, I held him against the wall. "What's your name?"

"Len. The name is Len. Not that it's any of your business," he spat.

His breath reeked of cigarettes and cheap whiskey and his ball cap had fallen off to reveal greasy, unwashed hair.

I spun him around and twisted his arm up behind his back, just on the cusp of pushing it too far.

"Let me go, you fucker!" he screamed.

I twisted it harder.

"Let me go, man," he begged, taking on a different tone. "Look, she's my long-term girlfriend. We were just having a misunderstanding. You know how that is. You gotta stay on top of these women. Otherwise they'll turn into whores."

While Len blustered, I looked around the room. It was littered with food wrappers and beer bottles. His clothes covered the floor, and a suitcase in the corner was opened to a small stack of neatly folded women's clothes. Bel had been figuratively and literally crammed into a corner.

And that pissed me off even worse.

"I want to let you know, Len, that you will never see Bel again. If you try to, your already pathetic life will come to a painful end. You don't want to test me. Do you understand?"

I let go of his arm, and he sank to the floor again, this time rubbing the arm I'd nearly broken.

I headed for the door. "Do we understand each other, Len?"

He screwed his face into something distorted and ugly. "Fuck you, asshole. That's my girlfriend. You can't just take off with her. She owes me money. That bitch owes me money for bringing her to Vegas and giving her a second chance at life."

He was not only a loser, but a delusional loser.

Len pushed himself to his feet and charged at me. Poor guy had no idea who he was dealing with. I grabbed him as he got closer and with the momentum he'd built, slammed him into the other wall, this time face first. He turned back to me, blood streaming out of his nose.

"She's mine, you fucker," he said, charging at me again.

Ugh. I hadn't wanted to get messy, but duty called. I planted my fist right in the front of his throat. He gasped and fell back, struggling for breath.

"Len. Let me tell you something a real man knows. A real man does not have to keep a woman under wraps. A real man does not have to control a woman. And a real man never, ever, HITS A WOMAN."

I stepped over him, resisting the urge to kick him in the balls. It was something guys normally never did to each other, even though this one sure as hell deserved it. But he was already down on the ground, incapacitated, at least for a while. That, along with my little talk about how a real man treats a woman, had delivered my message loud and clear.

Now it was time to deal with Bel.

10

ANNABEL "BEL" SIMMONS

"All my things are in the room. Sammy, I have to get my things."

Sitting in his car, I stared at my trembling hands, too ashamed to even look at him from the corner of my eye. And even as I said the words, I wished I hadn't. I was already pathetic enough, and asking to go back to that shithole to pick up the worthless junk I'd left behind would really drive home the sentiment.

If there were any question in Sammy's mind about what a loser I was, I'd say I just confirmed his worst fears.

He looked straight ahead as he drove his Mercedes, not even glancing my way.

He was disgusted with me. *I* was disgusted with me.

When he'd burst into the room and screamed at me to go, I'd run right down to Kate in the lobby, because where the hell else was I going to go? After she'd spent several minutes trying to calm me, Sammy appeared, blood on his hands and clothes, and took me to his car.

"Call me," Kate yelled.

I looked back over my shoulder and nodded.

I didn't know where he was taking me or why, or whether my situation was about to get worse or better.

In short, I didn't know a goddamn thing except I was getting queasier by the moment, and was having trouble breathing.

"I think I'm going to be sick," I whispered.

He screeched to the side of the road just in time for me to open the door. While I vomited, coughed, and sputtered so much I vomited again, he reached into the glove box and pulled out some napkins. He handed me several and used some to clean the blood off his own hands and jacket.

I sat in the car's doorway, head in my hands, taking deep breaths.

"It's understandable you got sick, Bel. What you just went through was pretty damn traumatic."

I glanced over my shoulder. His help was well intended, about that I had no doubt. But what the fuck? He just shows up and whisks me away? Was I in some sort of fairy tale?

Because I didn't believe in fairy tales.

And now that my head had cleared somewhat, I had questions.

I continued leaning out the car door. If I turned around, I'd have to face him. I wasn't ready for that.

Actually, I didn't know if I'd ever be ready for that.

For one sick moment I thought I'd have preferred staying with Len, putting up with his shit rather than have Sammy see me at my absolute lowest.

Pride was a dangerous thing.

"Bel, you need to understand that you can never see Len again. Never."

This time I whipped around to look at him. I was sure he wasn't serious. He couldn't be.

"What? Sammy, I am grateful for your help. But what do you mean I won't see Len again? Where am I supposed to go? Where am I supposed to live?"

I leaned back out the door, head in hands.

Finally, my most pressing question bubbled to the surface, dancing around since the moment Sammy had burst into the motel room.

"How did you find me? Why did you come to the motel?"

He didn't answer until I looked at him.

Extending his hand as if he wanted to take mine, he pulled it back just as quickly. "We... knew there was something going on, given the bruises on your arms. So the guys had me follow you home to suss out your living situation."

I took a deep breath. I was hoping the desert

evening's cool air might soothe my stomach, roiling over conflicting thoughts.

I was at once both grateful *and* angry for the way he'd stepped into my situation.

Seriously. In what world was it acceptable for an employer to follow an employee home and then dive into the middle of their home life—no matter how fucked up it was.

But I kept my anguish to myself. I had no idea where I was going to sleep that night, but I did know I'd be at my desk at BCL Enterprises bright and early the next morning. I needed that job and nothing was going to keep me from it if I had to sleep in the damn lobby.

I pulled the car door shut, certain that I'd puked up all my nausea, and clutched my purse to feel through the fake leather to the cash I'd hidden in the lining. That was my only comfort.

"Bel, the guys and I couldn't stand by and watch what was happening to you. My mother went through the same when I was growing up. When I see it happening again, I kind of lose my mind."

A harsh streetlight illuminated his hands, resting on the steering wheel.

"Len's going to be so mad—"

But he cut me off.

"Stop selling yourself short. You are a brave and strong woman. I see it in you. Don't let some loser take it away."

I leaned my head against the cool glass of the window. "I should have just stayed in West Virginia. I wish I'd never come to Vegas. I have no business here."

Sammy put his hand on my arm and my breath caught.

I hoped he hadn't noticed.

"You've got the three of us on your side now. Dom, Tristan, and myself. You're going to be fine. I'm taking you somewhere safe. Len won't be able to get to you. Ever."

At this point I had nothing left in me to argue, so I pulled on my seat belt and waited to see what he had in mind for me, which promised to be so goddamn safe Len would never find me.

His efforts were kind and while I hated to say this about one of my bosses—the man was full of shit. Len would find me. And I would pay.

"WHY ARE WE AT THE HOTEL?"

And why the hell were we coming in through the guest entrance? I'd only ever used the side entrance that led straight to BCL Enterprises.

Sammy put his car in *park*. A valet came running to open his door on one side and mine on the other. He left his keys in the ignition and walked over to collect me.

A chorus of, "Evening, Mr. Caputo," rang out like an echo.

I guess that's how it worked when you were the boss.

Sammy put a hand on the small of my back and hustled me toward the door. "We have a safe place for you to stay. You don't have to go back to that motel or Len. You don't deserve that shit you were putting up with."

Um, okay.

I wasn't sure what kind of world Sammy was living in, but in mine, you didn't just snap your fingers and make your problems go away.

No, in the real world, a gorgeous guy in a bitching Mercedes does not save you. He does not appear out of the blue, rough up your boyfriend, and then take you to a nice hotel where you could supposedly hide out and instantly start a better life.

He was either crazy or living in la-la land.

I stopped right before passing through the revolving doors. People streamed around us, barely noticing we were in the way.

"Sammy?"

He turned, his eyebrows raised. "Yes?"

I held my chin up. No way I was following an almost-stranger into a goddamn hotel, despite his being my boss. Or one of them.

I exhaled my nervousness. "What are you asking for in return? I have no money, and I'm not... for sale."

There. I'd said it. He might as well know. His big act of heroics did not guarantee him my body.

I was okay with putting up with Len's shit just a couple more weeks until I got paid. It wasn't enjoyable being with him, but at least I knew what to expect. He was an asshole, but a predictable asshole.

Fuck if I knew what I was walking into now.

And if Sammy didn't like that I wasn't trading myself for his fancy offerings, he could drop my ass off on the side of the road and never see me again. I'd find another job and a place to live. I'd done it before. I'd do it again.

He let out a big breath and scraped his fingers through his hair.

"Shit."

He led me out of the path of hurried guests over to a bench where people waited for taxis.

"Christ, Bel. I hadn't realized how this might look to you. I was just thinking about getting you out of that situation."

Sure, bud. Say what you want.

It was clear I wasn't convinced of his altruism.

"Look, we're putting you up in the hotel until you find a better place. You can stay as long as you want. We can offer you this because we own the place. But if you'd rather go elsewhere, I understand. It hadn't occurred to me that you might not feel safe here. I'd just... taken that for granted."

I stared at him.

"Dom and Tristan are inside, waiting for us. Let's talk, and if you'd rather go elsewhere, we'll help you with that."

"Sammy, why are you doing this? Why do you give a shit about my problems?"

He looked away from me, toward the chaos that was the front of the hotel, with the valets managing the cars and the bellmen towering stacks of luggage on their wheeled carts. Then there were the guests, who came in all shapes and sizes.

Something for everyone in Vegas, I'd heard it said.

"I... *we*... couldn't bear to see the bruises on you. We guys come from rough backgrounds. When this shit resurfaces in our lives, we put an end to it, because we can. And personally, I get really dogmatic about this stuff. I'm sorry I scared you. Hell, that's the last thing you need right now."

Well, shit. There was a hint of sadness in his tone.

He continued. "As I said before, my mom... went through something similar. This brings it all back. Now, I can do something about it, even if I do occasionally bumble. But this is about you. Not me."

My heart melted. A little.

"It's about what you need. And want," he added. "I can take you somewhere else. Just say the word."

I took a deep breath through my discomfort, and realized it wasn't going anywhere. And I was glad.

It kept me on my toes, cynical and suspicious. It helped keep my guard up. It just wasn't as high, now.

I stood and gestured toward the revolving doors that a moment ago I'd refused to enter. "C'mon. Let's go."

11

ANNABEL "BEL" SIMMONS

I FOLLOWED Sammy to the lobby, where we found Dom and Tristan.

I was now faced with the three men who were my new employers, who also happened to be acquainted with the indignity that was my personal life. As if this wasn't nerve-racking enough, I was also assaulted by the *ding-ding-ding* of the hotel's casino, the smell of something perfumey being filtered into the air to cover the smell of cigarettes, and the flurry of guests coming and going with their wheeled bags.

The lobby of a Vegas hotel and casino was not for the faint of heart.

Even though I'd had somewhat of a heart-to-heart

with Sammy, the second I saw Dom and Tristan, I was an employee again. I tucked my hair behind my ears and straightened my back. They might be offering me a helping hand, but it wasn't like we were friends. Not by a long shot.

Which further complicated my discomfort. They saw me as a charity case. I know they did.

"Bel. We're glad you're here," Dom said, his gaze drilling through me like it always did.

Damn him.

Tristan, in a suit like always, slipped the knot of his tie down and opened the top button of his dress shirt. "Yeah, Bel. Sounds like it's been a rough time. We hope we can offer you some… new options." His gaze gave nothing away. It was as if he were in a business meeting, negotiating something.

I didn't even look at Sammy. He'd seen the ugliness up close and personal. I could only imagine what he thought.

The three went silent, a clear indication it was my turn to say something.

Instead, I wished I could disappear into a hole in the ground. The shame was battering me, and their pity only intensified it. I wanted to chafe against it, but it was sitting on my chest, making it hard to believe.

I pushed it away. Like Tristan had said, this was about 'new options.'

"I… I don't know what to say. Obviously." I forced myself to look at each of them, one at a time.

Sammy held his hands out. "What do you say we show you the room we set aside for you. If you don't like it, or don't want to stay here at the hotel, then we'll work on a plan B."

Tristan raised his pointer finger. "However, there is no better hotel in Vegas. So if you want a downgrade, fine, but you'd be fucking crazy."

What was fucking crazy was that I was going from one of the worst shitholes in Vegas to a freaking palace with its marble floors, glittery chandeliers, and giant flower arrangements on pedestals taller than I was.

The contrast was dizzying.

And the shitshow of the day, coupled with the intensity of the hotel lobby was more than I could take. And I could take a lot.

Tristan took my arm. "Do you feel okay, Bel? You're pale."

I swallowed and wiped at the perspiration that had formed on my upper lip. "I would like to rest. Maybe have some water."

"All right. Shall we go up to the room? There'll be water there. And I'll call the hotel doctor."

Reluctantly, I leaned into Tristan and the four of us headed for the elevators that flanked each side of the lobby.

On the way up, Tristan carefully offered me support without being too handsy. I was still on my guard and would have accepted nothing less, unless he wanted a smack right across his cheek.

"You know," he said, "you're going to have a very short commute to work."

He looked at the other guys, who laughed.

I produced a limp smile. "Well, that's a good thing, because my… my boyfriend and I shared a car."

The word boyfriend made me feel like I might throw up again.

We headed straight for the room, which Dom opened with a key card, and before I even looked around, I plopped into the first chair I saw.

It was exquisitely comfortable, of course.

I leaned my head back and closed my eyes.

"Quite a day, huh," Dom said, taking the seat opposite mine.

Tristan handed me a bottle of cold water, which I chugged.

Wiping a drop off my chin, I took a deep breath. "Thank you. Thank you so much. I'll pay you back for this. Somehow."

Dom waved his hand. "No, you won't. Because this costs us nothing. Remember, we own the place."

Okay. Fine. They gave me a free room. I still wanted to pay for it. There must be some value on it. If there were guests in it, wouldn't the hotel be making money?

But the fact of the matter was, I would never be able to afford a suite much less a regular room in a hotel like this. I looked around and from where I sat saw at least two bedrooms, a small kitchen, and of course, the living room where we were sitting.

Who lives like this?

A knock on the door jolted me out of my thoughts.

God no. Could it be Len? I looked for a place to hide. I knew he'd show up. Sammy had said he'd never find me. But he didn't know Len. When he wanted something, his determination was relentless.

Instead, Tristan opened the door and stepped aside to let a small woman enter. She walked directly to me with an outstretched hand.

"Hi, Bel. I'm Doctor Ridley."

Oh. The doctor. Right.

That hadn't taken long.

"I don't think I need a doctor. I'm feeling fine now."

She continued smiling.

Dom walked to one of the bedrooms where he pushed the door wide open, gesturing for the doctor and me to follow.

"It will be a quick exam, Bel. We just want to make sure you're in tip-top shape."

I eyed everyone warily. There was no way I'd ever get used to this kind of treatment.

I followed the doctor into the room, where she pulled the door shut with the three guys on the other side of it.

"Have a seat, Bel," she said, gesturing at a loveseat in the corner.

She rifled through her bag and came back with a stethoscope and blood pressure cuff.

Basic. I was okay with that. But anything more was going to be a hard *no*.

While she listened to my heart and felt my neck, she got closer to the bruise on my face. She didn't say anything. I was sure the guys had already clued her in.

"Bel, you can press charges, you know."

"Excuse me?"

She reached into her bag and came back with alcohol and gauze. When she'd wet a piece of it, she began to dab it on the bruise on my face.

I jerked my head back. "That hurts."

She nodded. "I imagine it does. And now that I removed some of your makeup and can see the bruise on your cheek, I'll say again that you can press charges."

Like I didn't fucking know that.

She stepped back and looked at me. When several silent seconds passed by, she snapped her bag shut.

"From this quick exam, you seem to be in good health. Hopefully, your new home will take some of the stress out of your life."

Jesus. She knew everything.

"Thank you, Dr. Ridley."

We returned to the living room where the guys had made themselves at home drinking something on the rocks. I could bet it wasn't the cheap shit Len drank.

If this was to be my home for the near future, they weren't turning it into a guys' clubhouse, and I'd make sure they knew that. I'd put the chain on the door every time I was home.

Dom raised his glass. "We have a smiling patient. And doctor."

Ridley gave me a maternal look. "Can I share the results of your exam, Miss Simmons?"

I shrugged. "Sure."

She looked to the guys. "Bel is fine. Just a little too much stress."

Glass in hand, Dom rose and showed the doctor out.

But just before she left, she turned to me. "Think about what I said, Miss Simmons."

And she was gone.

Dom gathered the glasses and put them in the small kitchen sink, joining Tristan and Sammy at the door.

"Go ahead and get some rest. We'll see you tomorrow," Tristan said.

"Um, before you guys go, could someone give me a lift to a drugstore? I don't have any toiletries. Or I could take an Uber."

I needed not only toiletries but also something to wear to work. Actually, because I didn't have a stitch of clothing aside from what was on my back, I needed an entire wardrobe. Which, with some careful spending, I could probably get with the money stashed in the lining of my purse.

Tristan fake-slapped his head like he'd forgotten something, and Dom rolled his eyes at him.

"Right. There are basic toiletries in the bathroom. Make a list of everything else you need and we'll get it for you."

"I can't go out?" I asked.

"No," Dom said. "Not right away. We need to make sure you're safe. And Bel, don't tell anyone, even your best friend, where you are staying."

That wasn't going to be hard. I didn't really have anyone to tell since my one girlfriend at home had leaked my whereabouts once before. There was my sister, and Kate back at the hotel, but they didn't need specifics.

"Yeah, Bel, we need to… make sure Len is heeding our warning before you can roam freely and be sure he won't be bothering you. If he isn't, we'll take care of him."

A tingle ran up the back of my neck.

Take care of Len? What the hell did that mean?

I didn't want to know.

And what were these guys anyway? Hotel-owning thugs?

I closed the door after them and leaned up against it.

Holyfuckingshit.

What had just happened to my life?

I threw the deadbolt and put the chain on the door, and began to explore the suite slowly, still not convinced Len wasn't about to leap out from inside a closet or from behind a chair. I wanted to make sure there were no other entrances where someone might get in. When I found none, I pushed a heavy chair against the one door I'd just double locked. A girl couldn't be too careful.

When I was finally certain no one could get in without a squad of firemen, I walked over to a window that provided a sweeping view of the mountains in the distance, which were quickly fading in the setting sun.

Distant music caught my attention and I realized my suite overlooked the pool below. Even though it was evening, girls in tiny bikinis and guys in board shorts were down by the pool, talking, laughing, and splashing around.

How easy life looked for them. They were staying in an expensive hotel, hanging out by its sprawling, luxurious pool. They were a chic, good-looking bunch, having food delivered to their lounge chairs and tables, and ordering cocktails at the bar.

They were having fun. Something I hadn't done in a long time.

And if what the guys said was true—that they were offering me 'new options,' and that 'I could have a different life'—some fun would be nice.

I just wasn't sure I remembered how to have it.

12

TRISTANO "TRISTAN" LASTRA

"T‍HANK YOU FOR THE FLOWERS, T‍RISTAN."

Well. Who stood at my office door, but the lovely Bel.

Except I barely recognized her. Christ. Did one night in a nice hotel change a person that much?

"Good morning. You look… amazing."

Actually, she looked more than amazing. But I didn't want to drool over her. At least not in my office.

"Thank you. I love the flowers. And these new clothes came from Sammy."

She ventured in a few more steps looking a hell of a lot more together than she did the evening before.

The transformation was astonishing. And not just her appearance. She looked like the weight of the world had been lifted from her shoulders.

She was electrified. "You should have seen it, Tristan, someone came by my room last night with bags full of clothes. This bellman named Jim. I'm not kidding. I've never seen so much stuff. They were beautiful, every last piece, and they all fit. How did Sammy do that?"

She ran her hands over her new dress, smoothing the expensive fabric.

And how did I know the dress was expensive? Because we had bought it for her.

We didn't spend our money on crap.

And expensive looked good on her, as we knew it would. Her slim forest green dress was the perfect complement to her flaming hair, skimming her slight curves, and stopping just below her knees. Her sky-high pumps lengthened her already-long legs and a small cashmere sweater in nude, the same color as her shoes, topped it all off.

Only, she wasn't wearing the sweater for warmth—it was a hundred degrees outside.

She was covering her damn bruises.

But they'd be gone soon enough, just like the loser boyfriend. We had a team tracking his movements. He seemed pretty likely to try and find Bel, and if he got close enough, we'd intervene. That would not be a happy day for the creep.

We didn't use violence until we had to, even though many of our syndicate colleagues did without discretion. They'd catch up, eventually. The modern 'business' world required more finesse. I thought of it as 'twenty-first century arm-twisting.' In Dom's father's day, they literally twisted arms. Now, we did it figuratively. Mostly.

And got better results.

"I don't know how I'll repay you. These clothes are very expensive. And the flowers were just so incredible."

I waved my hand. "You're not repaying anything. Think of it as a springboard to a new life. People have given us guys opportunities, and we like to pay it forward. Maybe someday you'll know someone you can help."

Her eyes watered, but she quickly sniffed and cleared her throat.

"Absolutely. You're right. Pay it forward."

"So, tell me about the clothes," I said, gesturing at the chair opposite my desk.

She grabbed a seat, using animated tones and wild gestures. We'd done the right thing in helping her. She was appreciative. And happy.

"I was relaxing in my room wearing one of those wonderful hotel robes when someone knocked on my door. When I looked through the peephole, I saw it was Jim with one of those carts. He wheeled it in, unloaded all the bags, and handed me a note from Sammy. It said to set aside what I liked and didn't like, and that someone would be by to pick up the rejects. Can you imagine, calling clothes like these rejects?"

She looked at the ceiling and laughed.

That made me happy. And a little turned on, if I were honest.

She babbled on about trying on the clothes, and how afterward she slipped into a new pair of PJs and watched a romantic comedy.

The trauma of her day seemed far away. But *seemed* was the key. The shit she'd been through would never be far enough away.

"Damn, Bel," I said, teasing, "you got clothes and flowers all on the same day. I wish someone would do that for me."

She laughed. "Somehow I don't think flowers and dresses are your thing."

I was glad to see her more comfortable with me, and not just because I'd sent her flowers. I think she'd decided we guys were okay.

At least I hoped so.

"You're right, dresses and flowers are not my thing. But front row seats to a boxing match, or an expensive bottle of scotch are. In case you're going Christmas shopping."

"Oooh, I'll have to remember that. Say, Tristan, I'd like to ask for one more favor, if you don't mind. Can we keep all this between ourselves?"

Ah. She was learning.

"Yes. That's our preference too."

She hesitated for a moment, as if she wanted to talk. "Do you have a busy day ahead, Tristan?"

I didn't know if it was going to be busy as much as it would be frustrating.

"Not sure yet. We're having trouble at the pawn shops."

She scratched her nails over the fabric of her new dress, perhaps not entirely comfortable with me. "That's right. You run the pawn shops."

"I do. I started working in one of them a long time ago, when Dom's dad was still around. He liked my work ethic and promoted me."

"Dom's dad. He died a while back, right?"

"He did. Heart attack."

My office intercom buzzed and I reached for it, leaving it on speaker.

"Tris. Is Bel up there?" Dom asked.

I gestured for Bel to answer.

"Hi, Dom. Yes, I am, but I'm coming right down."

"Okay. I need your help with something."

The intercom clicked, and Dom was gone.

He wasn't one for unnecessary pleasantries. He hadn't grown up around them, and didn't see the point in pretending to be someone he wasn't.

He was different from other syndicate guys in that regard. But in all others, he was the same. Ruthless. Unforgiving. And vicious when the occasion called for it.

Which was why I needed to put an end to the goddamn pawnshop break-ins before he started bashing skulls, the number one thing on my mind lately.

Well, after the lovely Bel.

13

TRISTANO "TRISTAN" LASTRA

When I arrived at Dom's office for our daily afternoon meeting, I found Bel regaling Sammy and him with stories of the treats she'd received the night before.

Sammy was grinning ear-to-ear, having hit a home run. Dom just looked amused with her delight.

She waved at me and continued babbling. "Sammy, I would have been happy with stuff from the GAP. Seriously. That's where I'll go with the paycheck advance you guys gave me. That and Target."

Sammy held his hands up. "No, no, no. We can do better than that."

She laughed and shrugged. "Okay. If you insist.

Now, one more question before I let you guys get into your meeting. Just to make sure I understand Dom, you want me to call all the people on your list to invite them to your party, although we don't know the date or location yet. What if someone wants to know more about it?"

The corner of Dom's mouth turned up. He did this all the time. Invited people to an event without telling them anything about it. "Tell them if they want to know more, they have to fucking show up."

Yup. That was Dom.

A puzzled look crossed her face. I didn't blame her. How do you invite people to a party without a date and location? But it was Dom's game, not mine. "Okay. Got it."

We watched her leave, her little ass jiggling the tiniest amount under her dress. I knew I wasn't the only one in the group sporting wood.

Sammy shook his head when she closed the door. "We sure as hell made that one happy. Feels good, man." He sat back in his chair and puffed out his chest a little.

From practically dragging her into the hotel the night before, to her bright smile today, she'd come a long way. And Sammy was right, it did feel damn good. I liked helping people. People who deserve it, that is.

Dom gestured at my face. "So, Tris? You wake up late this morning?"

I scratched at my beard stubble. "Sure did. Spent

half the night jerking off to thoughts of a certain pretty girl."

"You've already got the hots for her, huh?" Sammy asked.

Dom smirked. "He sure as hell does. He sent her fucking flowers."

Shit. I'd wanted that to remain private.

But it was just as well they knew. "So what, man? She deserves them. You saw what a shit day she had."

The room was silent.

"*What?*" I snapped at them.

Dom raised his eyebrows. "I know we said we weren't going there with women we work with. But it looks like that idea is out the window."

I leaned back in my chair and stared at the expensive coffered ceiling Dom had installed after his old man died. He'd actually had our office ripped down to the studs, wanting to erase any remnant of the guy.

I hadn't thought his father so bad, but Dom was carrying a lifetime of hate. He wasn't one to forgive and forget. We'd grown up together and I'd witnessed his festering rage. It only began to subside when Dom got his hooks into his dad's business and forced the man out.

"You're not kidding. Hell, Sammy sent her a whole new wardrobe. I only sent flowers."

I was glad we were all on the same page. Bel was different than the usual women we met with their hands out and their entitled attitudes. Vegas was full of them.

I wasn't going to pitch the guys on my idea yet, but since we were on the topic of a pretty redhead, I went for it. "I'm just gonna say it, guys. I know we don't know her well yet, but I'm thinking about inviting her to our… arrangement. See if it's something she'd be down with."

Dom, who'd been looking out his window turned back to me, rolling his eyes. "She's not the type. No way. I can just see telling her we like to *share*."

We'd see about that.

"Well, what'd you learn about her, anyway?" Sammy asked.

He was interested. I only had to convince Dom.

"From the Midwest, no vices that I could find. Parents died young in a car crash where her alcoholic dad was wasted, she and her sister were brought up by an elderly aunt, recently deceased. She had good grades but an unstable home life which pretty much sucked away any opportunities a smart kid might have had."

Maybe this was why I had a hunch about her. I knew her story. It was one I'd seen before.

"There's one more thing."

They looked at me, waiting.

"She was arrested for shoplifting a seventy dollar item shortly before she came to Vegas. Charges were dropped, but it's still on her record."

Dom slammed a hand on his desk. "All right. So she does have a little badass in her. I like it."

Sammy laughed. "Dude. How do you find this shit out?"

"I told you. I *know* people. I have *connections*."

"But in fucking West Virginia? Do they even have electricity there?"

I should know better than to get sucked into Sammy's goading. "You're just being ignorant now. Mister sophisticated Vegas guy, are ya?"

"Hey, you know I grew up on the wrong side of the tracks, so don't pull any elitist shit with me."

"Okay, ladies, let's quit bickering. We have bigger fish to fry than the pretty lady sitting on the other side of my door," Dom said. "Who has a police record."

WE PULLED INTO THE RUTTED PARKING LOT OF A SHITTY old office park that hadn't seen its better days in probably twenty or thirty years.

Vegas had its off and on building booms, and sometimes the structures that resulted from the good times left little to be desired. When cash was flush among developers and permits were easy to get, shitholes like this were slapped up with no thought to how they might age. But hey, they offered cheap rent to businesses looking to maintain a low profile.

Like the illegal poker parlor we were about to pay a visit to.

"Joe. Good to see you," Dom said after we were buzzed in.

In this business, you always had to be buzzed in. Security was paramount, especially for someone like Joe, who dealt with large amounts of cash.

He sat back in his office chair, hands folded over his huge belly. He'd been a casino dealer for years, but got caught doing something illegal—what, I didn't know or care—so with no other options, he started operating his own under-the-radar card games. Problem was, it took a bunch of cash to get a small-time gaming operation going.

So he came to us. We had cash, and we made loans. Lots of them. It was a lucrative business.

But sometimes borrowers didn't feel like paying us back.

He figured he could sop up the poker players who'd been banned from legal games but didn't want to—or couldn't—stop playing. There were plenty of them around. It might have been a good, if illegal, business proposition if Joe didn't have his head up his ass.

"Hi, guys. To what do I owe this pleasure?"

His smile showed off yellowed teeth, and his office smelled like dirty ass. If he didn't get it together, his players would go elsewhere. The guys who came to this part of town didn't expect luxury, but they didn't want to sit in stench, either.

Dom scoffed at Joe's question. Like the man didn't know why we'd paid him a visit.

Actually, I had brought it up to the guys that we were wasting our time trying to collect what was, for our lending practices, a small amount of money. But they'd pointed out that in instances like Joe's, the perception of getting him to pay back his loan was almost more important than the actual money. If the street knew we were lax on collecting, everybody would be like Joe. In arrears.

And cavalier about it.

"Your payment is overdue, Joe. You know it is."

His eyebrows rose as fake surprise crossed his face.

His acting would win him no awards.

"Right. Right. Well, I have a big game tonight. I'm sure I'll have it after that."

Which meant he was essentially saying *fuck you*.

"Look, Joe. If you were honest and asked for a little more time, that would be different. But your current approach is only making things worse. Now, you know we have contacts at the gaming commission. I'm not saying this will definitely happen, but if by chance they found out what you were doing in this lovely little card room, you'd be faced with a felony. And I know that new young wife of yours won't stick around waiting for your sorry ass to get out of prison."

His face paled. "All right. I have some money in the safe. Let me pay an installment."

Asshole. I knew he had money on the premises. I

stole a look at Dom, who was bound to be pissed at Joe's attempt to mislead him.

"Joe, I suspect you could repay the entire loan right now, if you wanted to."

He looked nervously from one of us to the other. "But… but I need that cash for my game tonight."

Fucking weasel.

Dom leaned onto his desk. "I'll tell you what. I'm in a good mood. You get the money to us by noon tomorrow, and we'll get off your back. We won't even show you the photos we have of your hot wife boning the pool boy. Promise."

His face fell. Poor bastard was speechless. But did he really think a woman like his married him for his dick?

I led the way out of the office.

That's how things were done in the modern age.

14

ANNABEL "BEL" SIMMONS

"Mr. Bonetti ordered you breakfast."

I stepped aside as Jim wheeled a brass cart into my room, loaded with multiple covered dishes.

Jesus. How many people was he feeding with all that?

While the bellman laid all the dishes on the dining table, I lifted a couple domes to see what was on offer. The blissful smell of eggs and bacon filled the room.

There must have been ten separate dishes, not to mention a pot of coffee, orange juice, and ice water. "My god. This is breakfast? It looks like he ordered everything on the menu."

"I think he did. Here's a note." Jim handed me an envelope and headed for the door.

"Oh wait," I ran for my purse and pulled some cash out of the lining, where I was still hiding my money.

"Here you go. Thank you." I handed him a twenty. I actually had no idea what to tip a bellman

He smiled. "Thanks, Miss Simmons. See ya later."

I tore open the note.

Good morning, Bel. I wasn't sure what you liked, so I ordered everything. DB

These guys were full of surprises.

Food, clothes, shelter, and flowers. Pretty much all a girl needed.

I started pulling lids off the dishes and found French toast and pancakes, quiche, fruit, a couple egg dishes I couldn't identify, and a mound of bacon and sausages. I made myself a small plate and looked out the window at the pool below.

It was too early for the sunbathers and partiers, so the cleaning staff was vacuuming the pool, arranging the tables and chairs, and setting fluffy new towels out everywhere.

Maybe I could use the pool sometime.

What separated me from the folks picking up last night's drink glasses and hosing down sticky, sunscreen-covered lounge chairs?

There I was, on the twentieth floor of the swankiest hotel in Vegas, sitting in a thick white robe, surrounded by more food than I could eat in a month.

In a room full of flowers. Yes, Tristan had sent more flowers.

I looked around the suite at the bed I'd just gotten up from, covered in the softest cotton linens, to my closet filled with brand new clothes—things I never would have been able to afford myself.

How did I get *here*, and those people stuck in the endless tedium of cleaning the pool end up down *there*? I could easily be one of them. The guys could take all this away without notice, and I'd be back where I started.

Which wouldn't kill me. It might be disappointing, but I wasn't about to get used to this sort of life. There was no way it would last. I wasn't fucking stupid. And if I went back to where I'd started, so be it. I'd keep my chin up and deal.

But that didn't mean I wouldn't try my damnedest to improve my lot all I could. I'd gotten my first paycheck and practically run to the bank to open an account with it. I'd deposited every cent since, for the time being anyway, I was living rent-free. Cripes, I didn't even have to pay for my meals.

Yet.

The bottom could fall out. In fact, I was going to plan for it.

What would Len think if he could see me now? How about Kate, stuck behind the desk of that horrible motel? Or my sister, slaving away at multiple menial jobs to afford her college classes?

Len would be furious with jealousy. And I could not give a shit.

But Kate and my sister… they deserved better. Maybe they'd be my chance to pay it forward, like Tristan had talked about.

Yes. That would be my goal. To not only get myself into a stable situation, but be able to bring along my friend and my sister.

The first revelers arrived poolside, and I realized I'd lost track of time sitting around like a lady of leisure. Time for work. I dropped the muffin I'd been nibbling and ran for the shower. But the warm water coming out of the two showerheads in my marble bathroom embraced me like a warm hand.

And my own warm hand traveled down between my legs after I'd shaved myself smooth. I loved the way I felt when I was freshly bare, and then later, how my panties felt against my naked skin.

This time, however, my hand lingered as the faces of Dom, Sammy, and Tristan floated through my mind.

I hadn't known them for long, it was true. But they'd been so good to me, and they were so freaking gorgeous, I couldn't help but think about them… that way.

I imagined Dom entering the bathroom, dropping his clothes on the floor, and joining me under the warm water. My hand would immediately go to his hard cock, and he'd lean against the wall for balance, closing his eyes while shower water bounced off him.

He was so beautiful, his body glistening from the pounding spray. His muscles flexed from the tension of the pleasure I gave him, his neck corded around his Adam's apple. While I stroked him, I licked his dark nipples, my free hand tracing the thin line of hair leading to his erection.

"Fuck, baby," he murmured, rocking himself into my hand.

Just as Dom exploded on my stomach, the bathroom door blew open and Sammy walked in, followed by Tristan. They undressed and opened the shower door, handing Dom a towel as he exited.

Jesus. They were just as beautiful as Dom.

One of them got in front of me, the other behind.

"You're so wet down there, Bel," Tristan murmured, running his fingers through my slick folds. "Did jerking Dom's cock get you hot and bothered?"

"Ye... yes..." I gasped as Sammy pulled hard on my nipples.

"Did you like making him come all over you, nasty girl?" he whispered.

I could only nod. Thank god I was sandwiched between the two guys because I don't think I would have otherwise remained upright. I reached for Sammy's cock behind me, and Tristan's in front, each ready to please and be pleased.

I stood my feet apart and bent forward, directing Sammy's cock into my pussy while taking Tristan's in my mouth. Sammy stretched me to my limits but he took it slow and by the time he'd entered me completely, Tristan was banging against the back of my throat.

"Look at Bel," Tristan hummed. "Tag teamed by two hard cocks. How's that little pussy feel, Sam?"

He rocked harder, pushing my head into Tristan's stomach.

"She's tight, man, she's got a tight fucking pussy."

They continued to talk about me while I was bent over at a ninety-degree angle, sucking and fucking, like I wasn't even there.

And I loved it.

"What about you, Tris?" Sammy asked. "She sucking your dick good?"

"Oh, man. It's amazing. I'm gonna come fast, I can feel it."

Their dirty talk made me writhe even harder between the two, as if I were desperate and it was the last fuck I'd ever get. I was like a star in a porno movie, moaning without shame, begging for my orgasm.

And then it hit. Tristan unloaded in my mouth just as my pussy clenched and an explosion radiated from my core to every corner of my body. Sammy pumped me, with Tristan holding me up, until everything around me turned black.

I was gone. Done. Nonexistent.

The shower water began to cool, and I opened my eyes. I was alone, of course, having just gotten myself off. I wobbled out of the shower on trembling legs, grabbed a towel, and sat down for several minutes to catch my breath before I dressed for work.

To get to the office, I didn't even have to walk outside. The hotel was connected to a private hallway that led to the lobby of BCL Enterprises' office building. It was still a hefty fifteen-minute walk, and by the time I reached the elevators to head up to Dom's floor, I was breathless. But I had nothing to complain about.

Once in the mirrored elevator, I straightened my dress. It was probably on the slightly sexy side for the office with its low-cut neckline and slit up the thigh, but I didn't care. I felt good. I felt hot. I felt capable.

I was hoping Dom would give me something difficult to do today. I was up for a challenge and I wanted to show him—and the other guys—how I could handle anything they threw my way.

Like tag-teaming me in the shower.

Easy girl.

First order of business was to let Dom know I appreciated the insane breakfast he'd sent me, ninety percent of which was still on the table where the bellman had set it, waiting to be picked up by housekeeping.

I barged into his office for the first and last time.

"Dom, thank you for breakfast—"

But I stopped short.

He was with someone. A woman. Who was very beautiful. And didn't seem happy to see me.

Like the other women in the office, she looked me up and down, assessing everything about me from my hair to my shoes. So I did the same thing back to her.

"Sorry, Dom, didn't realize you were in a meeting." I turned and left, retreating to the safety of my desk.

Shaking.

Fuck. Why was I shaking? He was my freaking boss. Not my boyfriend, not my booty call, and not my shower fuck.

Just my masturbating fuck. Which was fine. I think.

I tried to push the beautiful woman out of my mind, and the way they'd both stared at me like I'd interrupted something important, and got to work lining up the catering for whatever mysterious party Dom was having.

I'd wondered more than once if I was going to be invited. I was sure I wouldn't be, but it was fun to imagine I was.

He'd told me next to nothing about his party, just like his guests. Why would the owner of a hotel and casino have such a secretive party? What was the big deal?

But that wasn't for me to ask, so I just ordered the menu Dom had requested, consisting of all sorts of high-end items like oysters, caviar, and champagne.

The funny thing was, I'd called the caterer and other

events folks and even though I couldn't tell them the exact date of the party or its location yet, they seemed completely unfazed. As if Dom did this all the time.

Maybe he did.

I was also a little confused about why the guys were paying me so much for a relatively easy job. I recalled Dom had told me his last assistant had retired to the Caribbean or something crazy like that with the bonuses she'd earned. Guess he paid all his assistants well.

And did that mean I might retire to the Caribbean someday?

Yeah, right.

But with the mystery surrounding Dom's 'event' as he called it, and his ability to pay so well, I had to wonder if they had some sort of business dealings not limited to the hotel and casino or pawn shops.

Shit, I hoped they weren't dealing drugs or something like that.

In the meantime, although I know I had no right to, I was dying to know who the woman in Dom's office was, and not because I'd just had the most intense fantasy about him and shower sex.

It was so strange. There was no reason for me to feel this way about him. Aside from helping me out— and well, sending me food and giving me a place to live —our relationship was strictly professional.

Right?

15

DOMENICO "DOM" BONETTI

"DID you want to talk to me, Bel?"

She looked up, a twirl of that sexy red hair hanging over her forehead. She tried to push it off her face but missed.

I wanted to help. I wanted to reach out and take that piece of hair, run it through my fingers, smell it, taste it, and tuck it back with her other hair.

Instead, I stared. And she stared back.

I'd been curious to know what she thought about my breakfast surprise. I'll admit it was a bit over the top, sending her one of everything on the menu. But you never knew what people liked for breakfast, just like Sammy didn't know what she liked for clothes.

Tristan guessed at what she liked for flowers, which wasn't hard because women liked all flowers given to them, even if they were freaking weeds.

Flowers were definitely safer than food or clothing.

"Yeah. I mean, yes. Thank you. For breakfast."

She turned back to her computer screen.

Okay, then.

"Bel?"

She took a moment, then looked back at me.

Jesus, did she have a bug up her ass.

I inhaled for patience. "Is something wrong?"

She pressed her lips together, then forced the fakest smile I'd ever seen. "No. Nothing's wrong. Nothing at all."

Eyes back to the screen.

For Christ's sake. I wasn't going to beg the woman to converse with me.

"It's almost time for lunch."

She realized what that meant, or thought she did, and reached for her purse. "What would you like today?" she asked, standing.

I tilted my head, taking her in. Her dress—one Sammy had chosen—was so fucking sexy I almost didn't want her walking down the street wearing it. I'd offer her a trench coat if it weren't so blasted hot outside.

Time to switch things up. "I was going to ask you what *you* would like."

That softened her a bit. She patted her stomach. "I'm still full from breakfast."

Good. Hopefully, she'd chowed. She needed to put a little meat on her bones. Not that she didn't look awesome, but a few curves would suit her perfectly.

"Okay then. We'll get something light. Do you like sushi?"

"Oh. Yeah. Love it."

I pulled some cash from my wallet. "I'll text you my order, that way you won't have to write it down. And get whatever you want for yourself. I like the restaurant Nobu. It's the best."

She took the money and headed for the elevator.

"Hey, my driver will take you. I'll call him to meet you in the parking garage. It's too hot to walk."

She was also too sexy to walk.

The elevator doors whirred closed.

"BEL IS ACTING STRANGELY TODAY. SHE WALKED IN ON me talking to Dede. Do you think she could be bent out of shape over that?"

Sammy wrinkled his nose. "Why should she give a shit if you were talking to your sister?"

I took a seat in his office as he opened a tin of Altoids. He popped those things like crack.

He held up a finger. "Unless… she didn't know Dede was your sister."

"Half-sister," I corrected.

He leaned forward and lowered his voice. "She likes you. That's what it is. She likes you."

He slapped his hand on his desk.

I shook my head. "Not sure about that."

"Regardless, we gonna start something with her?"

I rolled my eyes hard. "You tell me. You're the one who sent her all the clothes. And Tristan's been filling her suite with flowers."

The corner of his mouth turned up and I knew he was about to give me shit. So predictable. "What have *you* given her? And don't tell me nothing."

I was so done with this conversation. "I sent her breakfast this morning. "

Sammy held his hands up. "There ya go. She's beautiful, and for Christ's sake, she's on the hotel premises for work and home. It's hard for us not to think of her as more than your PA."

He was right about her being on the hotel premises, but wrong about her being beautiful.

That was understating it.

She was actually fucking stunning. And she never left my thoughts for more than a few minutes.

16

DOMENICO "DOM" BONETTI

Still preoccupied with whether Bel had gotten the wrong idea about my half-sister, I got back to my office to find her, having returned from Nobu, setting up my table for lunch. With two place settings.

Several boxes of sushi takeout covered my table, and she opened each one carefully.

"What did you get yourself?" I asked.

After she'd dumped the wasabi, soy sauce, and chopsticks on the table, she looked in the bag as if something were missing.

"I got the same as you." She took the seat next to me, which also happened to be the only seat available.

And not by accident.

Folding her hands in her lap, she waited for me to start. Still avoiding my gaze.

So, with my chopsticks, I put a few pieces of hamachi and maguro on my plate and mixed my wasabi and soy sauce in the exact proportions I liked.

Spicy but not too spicy.

And Bel continued to sit with her hands in her lap.

I waved at the abundance of food before us. "Take whatever you want. There's enough for ten people here."

I popped a piece of hamachi into my mouth.

Heaven.

I loved raw fish. Like *I could eat it every day of my life* loved it.

Bel picked up her chopsticks, which immediately tumbled out of her fingers. Frowning, she tried again, this time managing to keep them in place, but unable to manipulate them well enough to pick up food.

She didn't know how to use chopsticks.

Which was fine.

But she also didn't know not to put too much spicy wasabi in her soy sauce.

That's a mistake you only make once.

But I didn't want to embarrass her. In fact, I was going to help her save face.

It was my guess she'd never had sushi in her life. Thus, why she ordered the same thing as me.

I threw down my chopsticks like I was mad at them. "You know what? These things are a pain in the ass."

I got up and returned with two forks. "I'm going to use these. It will be so much easier."

Relief washed over her.

Tentatively, she speared a California roll and dipped it into her soy sauce. But before I could warn her about how hot it would be, thanks to the mound of wasabi she'd dumped into it, she popped the roll in her mouth and started chewing.

In seconds, her eyes watered and she began to sputter.

"The wasabi's hot, isn't it?"

She nodded and with tears running down her face, swallowed the rest of her roll without even chewing it. She reached for her bottle of water and drank half of it.

I would have found the whole scene was hysterical if it were anyone other than Bel. But she was trying so hard.

I pushed the white rice toward her. "Eat some of this. It will help put out the fire."

She looked at me hopefully and shoveled a huge forkful of rice into her mouth. Closing her eyes, she sighed as the burning diminished.

After a minute, she dabbed at her eyes and sweaty forehead.

God, she was cute.

Then, she coughed and blew her nose. "Oh my. Wow. That was something."

Fuck, I was dying to kiss her.

She popped another California roll in her mouth,

this time with no wasabi, and moaned. "Mmmm. I like this."

Her shitty mood was disappearing. Good sushi will do that to you.

So I made my move. I kissed her. Nothing long, dramatic, or seductive. Just something I'd wanted to do since the first time she came into my office for her interview. I'd known I was going to hire her, dispensing with the stupid questions from human resources.

Her smile told me she was pleased by my kiss. Nice.

She pressed her lips together and took a deep breath. "I have a confession to make."

"Hmmm?" I asked, popping some maguro into my mouth. Was she going to tell me about her police record?

"I've never... actually had sushi."

No shit.

But I wasn't making a big deal out of her lie. "How do you like it?" I asked, chasing my maguro with some rice.

"I like the rolls. I'm not sure about that stuff though." She pointed at the sashimi.

I got it. Sashimi wasn't for everyone. Most people I knew who were on the fence about sushi stuck to the rolls, where a mouthful of rice diluted any overwhelming fish taste.

I reached for the chopsticks I'd set aside and chose the smallest piece of hamachi, which was relatively mild-flavored. I dipped it in *my* wasabi-soy concoction, and held it to her mouth.

She turned her nose up. "Oh no. I don't like that green stuff."

"It's called wasabi, and if you mix only a small amount with the soy, it enhances the flavor."

She looked doubtful.

I directed the fish toward her mouth. "C'mon. Open up."

Now my dick was hard.

With her gaze fixed on mine, she parted her lips just enough to take the hamachi, and snatched it out of my chopsticks like a hungry cat.

After a moment, she closed her eyes and nodded. "Oh my god. This is good. Weird but good."

I loved it when I could introduce someone to sushi who truly liked it.

With a little sake and some candlelight, this could actually be a damn hot date.

And even though it wasn't, I kissed her again.

It was another quickie. Chaste, almost. Like a *testing the waters* kind of kiss. I pulled back before I couldn't stop myself.

Blushing, she smiled again.

I went back to my lunch. It wasn't easy, but I knew not to push.

And fuck that *no women from work* rule. I wasn't denying myself. If Bel wanted to experience all we had to offer, I'd be first in line to accommodate her.

And the guys would be right there, too, I had no doubt.

Yeah, we three had an unusual outlook on relationships. We *shared*. Not that Bel needed to know that.

Yet.

"I didn't get to introduce you to my sister this morning. Too bad she was in such a hurry."

Bel's head snapped in my direction. "That woman was your sister?"

I nodded. "Actually, half-sister. Her name is Dede and she's a singer. Next time she stops by I'll be sure to have you meet her. I don't see much of her these days, her career is really taking off."

And just as I'd hoped, something in Bel's posture relaxed a bit. Which was good because I was about to drop a little bomb on her.

"There's something else I wanted to talk to you about."

She set her fork down. "What's that?"

"Like a lot of employers in this age of technology, we monitor our employees' email."

I stole a look at her and, predictably, she was turning pink. Again. With her red hair and fair skin, there was probably nothing she could get away with.

"Look, you're not in trouble or anything. I just wanted to tell you I read what you emailed your sister about me. And the other guys."

Yup. She was so red I thought she might explode.

She had nothing to be ashamed of. So what if she'd

told her sister she was working for guys she thought were good-looking? And single? And generous? And who she imagined might have big dicks?

It was harmless, and I didn't care. But I wanted her to know we read that shit before she said even more to embarrass herself.

"I… I'm sorry. I hadn't realized…" she stammered.

I sighed. "Bel. It's okay. You're not in trouble. I just wanted you to know so you didn't continue putting personal stuff in your emails. It's fine that you keep in touch with your sister. Seriously. Just know we can read your shit. And we do."

I went back to eating because I had no doubt she wanted to crawl under the table and hide. It was the least I could do to look away and give her a moment to recover.

"Bel?"

"Yes," she mumbled.

"Do you like me?"

I knew I was putting her on the spot. But fuck all, I wanted to know where I stood.

Instead of answering, she popped to her feet and began gathering the empty sushi boxes. Then she grabbed everything that was left and consolidated it into one container. She piled it all on a large serving tray, including our dishes, wiped the table down and made a dash for the door.

And as she did, I could see the outline of her thong panty through her snug dress. I'd have to give

Sammy my compliments later on his choice of lingerie.

I'd pushed her. I knew that. But it was fine. She fucking liked me and it was just a matter of time before she was ready to admit it.

And do something about it.

17

ANNABEL "BEL" SIMMONS

ARE YOU GONNA FUCK HIM?

Shit, shit, shit.

Before I even ditched the fishy-smelling lunch dishes in the kitchen, I sprinted to my desk to delete any emails I'd stupidly sent to my sister about the guys. Actually, I deleted all our emails. They didn't need to know any more about my life than they already did.

No more emailing from my work computer.

Oh god. Had I mentioned my shoplifting gig, or my police record in an email? If I remembered correctly, Maggie had asked what the status of everything was.

And as I scrolled up to the very last one, where my sister was inquiring whether I was going to fuck one of the guys and if so, which one, I had to say I'd really outdone myself in the humiliation department.

Not only did the guys know I was musing about doing the nasty with them, but Dom also now knew that I'd never had sushi, and had been compelled to lie about it like I was embarrassed.

God, I could be an idiot.

When I'd seen only chopsticks and no other eating utensils fall out of the Nobu bag, I knew I was in trouble. We didn't have sushi places in the town where I came from, and the sole Chinese restaurant only provided forks.

I'd noticed while waiting for my take-out order that the patrons at Nobu used chopsticks like they were born with them.

Yeah, that wasn't in the cards for me. The guys must think I'm such a freaking hick.

And yet they still seemed to like me. It was all so inexplicable.

Las Vegas, and actually our entire office, was full of beautiful, sophisticated women who knew how to dress, act, and probably use chopsticks, too. I'd never fully understand why the BCL Enterprises guys had taken a liking to me.

But I wasn't complaining. No, I was going to ride this fucking wagon until the wheels fell off. I'd been given the chance of a lifetime to get ahead—and maybe have some fun at the same time—and planned to milk it all I could. This might never happen again. I knew that much. I'd grown up around people who never got chances, and the few I'd seen who did, usually blew it by taking them for granted.

But did my opportunities include kisses from Dom? And if so, why had I gone running out of his office like my ass was on fire when he asked if I liked him, like I was in sixth grade again or something.

The man knew I liked him, and he kissed me. Why is that such a big deal? I'd played with myself in the shower that morning imagining him doing a lot more than that.

What if he never kissed me again?

"Heard you had sushi for lunch, Bel."

I bet he'd heard more than that. Like how I nearly killed myself

"I did, Tristan. My first time. I liked it."

Time to be honest. I wasn't going to pull anything over on these guys.

He turned to head into Dom's office for their usual meeting.

"Hey, Tristan," I called after him.

"Yeah?"

"Do you have a moment for a question?"

He stuffed his hands in his perfectly pressed trouser pockets and nodded. "Sure. What's up?"

I hoped I wasn't going to offend him, but I had

something I had to understand. "Isn't gambling a big waste of money? I walk through the casino every day now. There are always so many people playing."

He looked at me for a moment. "I can understand why you'd ask that." He propped his butt on the corner of my desk.

"Gambling is entertainment, like going to a concert or ball game, or even traveling or owning a boat. Those cost money, too. So, if you say gambling is a waste of money, then you'd be saying all forms of entertainment are a waste. Know what I mean?"

Good point. I was glad I'd chosen him to ask.

"I hadn't looked at it that way." I swiveled in my desk chair, prickly from his nearness.

He smelled of a light but spicy aftershave. It was so subtle I almost had to lean closer to get a better hint of it.

"You know what, Bel? How 'bout I take you to the casino and show you how some of the games work?"

My heart thumped in in my chest. Oh my god. Hanging out with Tristan, the man who looked like he walked out of the pages of *GQ*.

"Um… yeah. That would be great. Thank you."

He headed for Dom's door. "I'm going into my meeting now with the guys, but when we're done, we'll go, okay?"

"Well, I don't know if I should go during business hours. I have work to do."

He laughed and waved his hand. "Consider this part

of your training. If you're PA to a guy who runs a hotel and casino, you should probably know a couple things about gambling."

He disappeared into Dom's office as Sammy rushed in, late as usual, pulling the door shut behind him.

They always closed the door when they spoke. Maybe all businesspeople were like that. I had nothing to compare it to.

But this time, the door didn't catch, and it was left hanging open a couple inches. I got up to pull it shut when I overheard something.

"The guns are late," Sammy said.

Someone slammed his hand down on the desk.

Guns? What about guns? Like guns for hunting? Or for self-protection?

"We have millions riding on this deal. If the Russians have fucked with our shipment, they're dead," Dom growled.

The sushi I'd had for lunch suddenly wasn't sitting well in my stomach. I silently closed the door. I didn't want to hear any more.

They had millions riding on a shipment of guns, and would kill someone who got in the way of it.

I'd been wondering about their businesses.

Now I had my answer.

18

ANNABEL "BEL" SIMMONS

"Bel, ready to go down to the casino?"

Having finished their meeting, all three guys stood at my desk. Guess they were done talking about guns and killing Russians.

I wanted to tell Tristan no. I didn't want to hang out with people who handled problems by killing people. I'd been around enough tough guys in my life, I didn't want to spend time with more, even if they were rich and good-looking. And gave me a place to live. And fed me. And clothed me.

How fucked was my life?

Dom slapped Tristan on the back. "Great idea, Tris.

Go ahead, Bel. This man is the best card player out of us all. Maybe he'll teach you some of his tricks."

He turned and went back into his office, this time closing the door all the way. Sammy took off for the elevator, pulling his shirtsleeves down and covering his tattoos.

Did they know I'd heard something? Was I in danger? If they talked about killing Russians so cavalierly, it would be nothing for them to take me out, too. Maybe that's why they had me staying on the premises —so they could off me any moment they felt like it.

But why would they have bought me all those clothes? And why would Dom have kissed me?

I pushed through my illogical, muddled thoughts and got to my feet. "Okay. But I have no money to spend on gambling."

As if that would get me off the hook.

Tristan just smiled.

Yeah, I had money hidden in the lining of my purse, but I wasn't about to piss that away. It might be just another form of entertainment for some, but it was nothing I was about to spend my precious money on.

Reaching into his pocket, Tristan retrieved a wad of rolled up bills. He peeled a couple off and thrust them at me.

Holy shit, they were hundred dollar bills. Benjamins. Hundos.

I thrust them back at him. "I can't take this. Thank you, though."

He closed my fingers around the cash and pushed my hand back. "Just say thank you, and accept it. Now, c'mon."

Without a word, and with the crumpled bills in my hand, I followed him to the elevator and down to the casino floor. I folded the bills tightly into my palm so I didn't look like a kid who'd just gotten their allowance.

First, we passed what Tristan referred to as the 'slot' games, the brightly lit machines screeching for passersby to stop. I walked by these noisemakers every day. I didn't get it. Rows of people sat on stools, pushing buttons and pulling levers—over and over and over. How could this be entertaining?

We walked until we reached a quieter part of the casino where people sat at tables headed by dealers in bowties, being served drinks by scantily clad waitresses.

I watched one drop off a beer to a man playing at a table alone. He didn't offer a tip, and she sulked away, looking for someone else to serve.

I could have ended up just like her. Actually, I still could. I knew opportunities came and went.

I was back to wondering why the guys chose me, instead of someone like her. I was certain she'd rather work in a nice quiet office like I did, wearing pretty clothes and having lunch with the boss.

And being kissed by him.

It had been weird being kissed by my boss. But

nothing else in my life was normal lately, so I tried not to overthink it. I'd only drive myself crazy if I did.

I preferred to think of it as lucky. I was lucky to be where I was at the moment, and I wasn't about to look a gift horse in the mouth.

But luck was not the sort of thing that's doled out fairly in life. So maybe it was just my turn for a little taste of it?

We walked through what felt like miles of tables, startlingly silent after the cacophony of the slots, and walked up to a roped off area with a sign reading *Private*.

Well, then.

Tristan moved the rope so we could enter and when he did, the gaze of every dealer flashed up at him. With discreet nods, they went back to their work moving around cards and colorful chips for the laser-focused players.

"What's this all about?" I whispered to Tristan.

He leaned next to my ear and if I wasn't mistaken, peeked down my dress for a split second. "This is where the 'high rollers' come," he said, using finger quote marks.

"What do you mean? Do they have to pay to get in?"

He shook his head. "Not exactly. But at these high stakes tables, each bet has to be a minimum amount. Some tables require one hundred dollars, all the way up to a thousand. But in the private salons up on the fiftieth floor, players have to prove they have a bankroll of no less than three hundred thousand just to get in."

My mouth dropped open. "You mean people actually come here to play with that kind of money? Like they could lose it all and be okay with that?"

He laughed. "They could win, too. That's why they come. In fact, it's said that the moment of *making* the bet—taking the risk—is more euphoric than even the actual win."

"That sounds… totally creepy," I said, wrinkling my nose.

Which I instantly regretted. Had I really just criticized the business of the company I worked for?

To save myself, I put on a bright smile and bounced up and down in my new stiletto heels. "Shall we try one? Which is best to learn on?"

He took my elbow and steered me toward a table with no other players.

"Mr. Lastra," the dealer said, putting his hands flat on the table.

What was that all about?

"Simon. This is a new employee, Bel. I told her I'd show her a little about playing Blackjack. If anyone else comes, would you tell them the table is closed?"

"Of course sir," he said politely, waving over a cocktail waitress.

Tristan ordered us both sparkling water.

Moving his chair closer to mine and with his head tilted my way, he began to explain that first you get yourself some chips, then you place your bet, then you get two cards. As we moved through the first hand, and I absorbed that you did your best to get as close as possible to a total of twenty-one, my hands shook. After all, I'd handed the dealer one of the hundreds that Tristan had given me, and now had a huge pile of chips.

"Tristan?" I whispered. "What if I lose all your money?"

He chuckled. "The first rule of gambling is not to bet what you can't afford to lose. I think of what I gave you as my 'play money.' If you win, great, and if you lose, that's okay too."

A modicum of relief passed over me, but as I reached to organize my chips out of nervous energy, I managed to knock my glass right off the table.

"Oh my god," I said, jumping off my stool to collect the ice cubes rolling around the floor. "I'm sorry."

Tristan took my arm and pulled me back to my feet. He gestured toward a staff member who was rushing our way with a broom and dustpan. "Sweetie, we have people to clean this stuff up—"

Sweetie? Tristan had just called me sweetie?

As I returned to my stool, I noticed someone familiar walking through the casino, staring right at me. But when I looked again, he'd turned a corner and was out of sight.

It was Len.

At least I thought it was Len.

Holy fuck.

"Bel, are you okay?" Tristan asked, helping me onto my stool.

I nodded, even though I was anything but. If Len had found me, there was no telling what would happen.

"I think I'm a little tired. This was super fun," I said through a forced smile. "Mind if we continue another time?"

"Sure. No problem. Let's get back to the office."

He dropped the leftover chips in his pocket after tipping a couple to the dealer, and kept his elbow on my arm as we backtracked through the casino.

I walked as closely to him as possible, trying to process whether or not I'd really seen Len, and whether or not Tristan had really called me sweetie.

It was entirely possible I'd imagined both.

19

SAMUELE "SAMMY" CAPUTO

"WHY DON'T you join Tristan and me for a drink, Bel?"

She looked up from her computer. "Hi, Sammy."

In place of her usual peppy expression were blood-shot eyes and a grim mouth. It looked like she'd lost her best friend.

Hell, maybe she had. All the more reason to join Tris and me. I wanted to hear about her gambling adventure.

I looked at my watch. "C'mon. Grab your stuff. I need to hit one of the bars downstairs to see how the new manager is doing."

She wrinkled her nose. "I'm kind of tired, Sammy."

She did look tired, in which case I was definitely dragging her out for a drink.

"We won't keep you out. Think of it as part of your job, checking out all the businesses we run."

Her chest heaved with a big sigh and she clicked off her PC. "All right."

She stood, her shoulders slumping, unfortunate because her dress rocked her slim figure and showed off her tits to maximum advantage. How could you be sad when you looked like that?

Easy for me to say. I hadn't been through the trauma she recently had with the abusive boyfriend, and then being moved to a new home that wasn't exactly of her choosing. I was sure she liked where she was—there wasn't much one could complain about—but in the end she'd had little say in the matter.

We settled in at the newest bar BCL Enterprises had opened in the hotel. The space had previously been a swimwear shop or something silly like that, one of the vestiges left from Dom's dad. We'd turned it into a bar and restaurant as soon as we had the permits to do so.

Serving alcohol was way more profitable than selling bikinis.

"So, what did you think about gambling? Tris told me he showed you Blackjack."

She nodded and sipped the white wine the bartender had dropped off. So far, from what I could see anyway, bar operations looked pretty smooth. As they should. We hired the best teams in the city.

"I can see why people enjoy it," she said politely.

"I get the feeling you don't completely approve of gambling."

She blushed. "Well, um… you're sort of right. You see, the boyfriend—I mean the guy you got me away from—came to Vegas to make it big playing poker. He lost all his money. So he was pretty much sponging off me."

Ah ha. I suppose I wouldn't like gambling if it had fucked up my life, either.

"Gambling isn't for everyone. For every person I know who's made some money from it, I know ten more who have lost theirs. Where it gets dangerous is when someone puts everything on the line. The chances of beating those odds are almost zero."

She nodded. "Like Tristan said, only bet what you can afford to lose."

"Exactly. Problem is, not everyone follows that rule."

"Hey, guys," Tristan said, grabbing the barstool on Bel's other side.

He waved the bartender down. "You guys want to join me in a scotch?"

I jiggled the ice in mine. "I'm ready for another."

"I'm good," Bel said, holding up the wine she'd barely started to sip.

"Do you prefer something else? Doesn't look like you're enjoying that," Tristan said.

She ran her elegant fingers up the stem of her glass.

"Actually, I'm just trying to make it last. It's really good. Most alcohol I've had has been terrible, cheap stuff."

I liked seeing Bel seated between Tristan and me. Something about it was a turn on. Like she might someday really be sandwiched between the two of us.

Even though we weren't supposed to do shit like that with employees.

"Since I have you both here together, I wanted to tell you something." She looked straight at her wine glass instead of either of us.

Tristan sipped his scotch and nodded at me, letting me know he approved of the brand we'd decided to carry. "What's up?"

She took a deep breath. "So, today when I was getting my blackjack lesson, I didn't say anything because I was too freaked out, but I'm pretty sure I saw Len in the casino. The guy I was… staying with at the motel."

So that's why she looked so down in the dumps. I couldn't blame her. No woman would want to be haunted by a loser like that. But she had nothing to worry about with us on her side.

"How sure are you, Bel?" I glanced at Tristan, who was as concerned as I was.

"Pretty sure. I mean, not one hundred percent, but pretty sure. And now it's all I can think about."

She seemed so vulnerable. And anxious. Which I didn't like at all.

In fact, I was getting pissed.

"I'm glad you told us that, Bel. I told that fucker not to come looking for you."

Tristan nodded. "You should have told me when you saw him, Bel. I could have checked things out. But I know you were scared. The last thing we want is for you to be scared."

Appreciation washed over her face as her eyes filled with tears. That guy had really done a number on her. And it was time to put a stop to it. He had no business fucking with her, and by default, us.

"Thank you," she said quietly. "Now I have one other thing to ask."

"Nope. Sorry. You've used up your quota for questions."

Tristan looked at her very seriously until she figured out he was kidding.

"Very funny. So, what I was going to ask, um... was about your business. I heard you guys talking about guns the other day?"

Well, shit. Not sure how that happened, but I liked that she had the balls to ask about it.

I looked at Tristan, who was surprised by her forthrightness. I, however, was not. I knew she had it in her.

"Since you asked, I'll tell you. But this requires the loyalty Dom told you we expect from people."

She looked at me expectantly, and fuck if she wasn't beautiful with those red tendrils falling around her face.

"Okay."

"Dom, Tris, and I run some activities for a local syndicate."

She frowned and the cutest lines between her eyebrows deepened. "What does that mean?"

"That means… in addition to the hotel, casino, restaurants, and bars like this one, as well as the pawn shops, we engage in some activities that you might say… skirt the law."

She opened her mouth to speak, but seemed to think better of it. Then she exploded with her question, whispering. "Is that like organized crime? Like the mafia?"

She'd put that together fast.

"Yeah. Pretty much."

Her eyes grew wide as she processed the new information.

At the same time, Tristan reached for his phone while I focused on Bel. She had a lot to learn. Hopefully as she did, she wouldn't be inclined to run in the opposite direction.

"Shit," Tristan said, downing the last of his scotch. "One of the pawn shops was just knocked over again."

Goddammit. I thought we'd put that problem to rest.

"Why do they keep getting robbed?" Bel asked.

"They have a lot of cash and expensive merchandise that people have pawned."

Her eyes widened.

"I'm going to get my car out of the valet. Meet me out front," Tristan said, and took off.

"Well, damn. I'm afraid, Miss Bel, that we are going to have to cut short our little happy hour."

She looked around, her eyes full of fear.

So I put a hand on her arm to comfort her. "Don't worry. I'll clue the bartender in. He'll keep an eye on you and call one of my bellman friends to walk you to your suite."

"Really? Are you sure?" she asked, her eyes darting about.

"Completely sure. Now, please try to relax. Enjoy your glass of wine."

I stood to go.

"I can pay the check," she said, gripping her purse.

Was that what she was worried about?

"No need. We own the place. Remember?" I reached into my pocket and threw a fifty on the bar.

"What's that for then?" she asked, still on alert.

"Tip for the bartender. He has a big job in looking after you. We aren't letting anything happen to you, Bel."

She relaxed a little and gave me a small smile.

I'd take whatever I could get.

"You're scared, aren't you?" I asked, leaning closer to her.

I knew I shouldn't, but there was just no stopping.

She tried to look brave. "I am. Off and on. Sometimes I think everything will be fine, and sometimes I think Len will find me. If he does, it would be bad, Sammy. Really bad."

It killed me to see her so shaken by that fucker. We'd take care of him as soon as we could.

Without even thinking about it, I pulled her to me, and damn if she didn't smell wonderful. I shouldn't have, but the urge to protect her overran any propriety.

"I'm sorry, Bel. So sorry you have to go through this. But we guys will take care of it. I promise."

I leaned back to see her eyes. She was so beautiful and vulnerable and I found myself vowing to do anything I could to protect her. But in that moment, all I could think about was kissing her.

So I did. And her lips melted under mine in a connection that I hoped made her feel safe. She deserved it.

20

SAMUELE "SAMMY" CAPUTO

"Who's the lovely redhead you guys have been seen around town with?"

Wow. This fucker must have a death wish.

I cracked the butt of my gun across his face and he fell to the floor, blood streaming from his nose and the fresh gash on his cheek.

So much better than using my fist.

I liked to try to save my hands whenever I could. All us guys did. I was usually restrained in meetings like this, but the asshole had blown it when he brought up Bel.

"You fucker," he screamed, cupping his nose.

"You ever mention her again, Damian, or even look

151

her way, you're dead. Do you understand that? We'll maim the shit out of you for knocking over our pawn shops, but even thinking about her will get you six feet under."

He looked up from the floor, smiling through the blood, swelling, and what was probably a broken nose. "Wouldn't it be terrible… if something happened to her?" he taunted. "And you know, I've always had a thing for redheads. Especially if the carpet matches the drapes."

This time, Tristan caught his dress shoe in the man's face. He screamed again and fell backward, his face a grotesque distortion of what it had been only ten minutes before.

Tristan wiped the blood off his shoe. "Just for that, scumbag, you'll not only find yourself six feet under, but your pretty wife will be right next to you, pushing up daisies. Now open your goddamn safe and return the jewelry and cash your goons took."

The thought of this lowlife even looking at Bel angered me until I couldn't see straight. I had half a mind to just off him right there, but Tristan and Dom wouldn't have liked that. We all knew I was the hothead of the group, and they did their best to temper me. After all, we had a reputation to uphold. They liked to draw the process out and create a little noise. Offing someone right off the bat cut all that short, and so was a last resort. They liked for the rest of the folks who might fuck with us to see the consequences of doing so.

I grabbed Damian by the upper arm and dragged him to his safe. He turned the dial several times, reached in, and threw a yellow bag at me, staggering back against the wall and groaning.

I needed to focus. Control my rage. "You hit one of our shops again and I will make good on my promise to you, Damian. Don't doubt it."

We took the bag and left.

"Jesus, Sammy, that was quite the reaction you had, when he mentioned Bel," Tristan said, steering away from Damian's shithole of an office.

He was right, and I was kind of stunned myself. It was like something had come over me when he'd said her name. And hearing he'd use her to hurt us had pushed me right over the edge.

Further amplifying everything was the fact that I had taken a liking to Bel—I wasn't going to lie about it. I hoped I'd scared him.

Because I scared myself.

"WHAT EXACTLY IS A CHEF'S TABLE?"

The elevator from Bel's floor to the hotel lobby was moving entirely too fast. I wanted it to slow, or even stop altogether.

Finally, it was just the two of us in a confined space. I could look at her without distraction. But because it would have been fucking weird to stop the elevator and just stare, I drank her in all I could during the brief time that I had. Sure, I'd be with her for a substantial part of the evening, but I somehow felt she was more *mine* when no one else was around.

And drinking her in was something I could get used to doing, as frequently as possible.

She was wearing one of the dresses I'd chosen for her, a silky black number that screamed against her pale skin. Her curly red tresses fell around her shoulders and back like ribbons on a birthday present.

And she was like a birthday present. Exciting, anticipated, and wanted. Desperately.

I'd gotten dressed up too, actually putting on trousers and a sports jacket. I could pull it together for someone special.

"Top chefs often have a table or counter in the kitchen where people can sit, watch what's going on, and get served special dishes."

She raised her eyebrows as we exited the elevator. "That sounds so strange. Like why would you want to sit in the kitchen when you could have a perfectly nice table in the dining room?"

She had a point.

I put my hand on her lower back, forcing restraint. "It's a weird status-y thing, to sit in the kitchen of a high-end restaurant and be served. I get that at first glance it might not sound that appealing, but people get off on having face time with big-name chefs. You know, it's like *being with the band*."

She shrugged. "Okay. I get it now. It makes people feel important, like they're members of an exclusive club. It sounds fun."

As we took our seats at a small table in view of the head chef, Bel scooped up the bottom of her dress to avoid dragging her chair over it. Her movement was so elegant and sexy at the same time, I was immediately sporting wood. Fortunately, I was seated before it was noticeable.

"So the chef has decided the menu, and he worked with the sommelier on a wine pairing."

Confusion crossed her adorable face. "Wine pairing? Like the fruit?"

"*Pairing.* Not *pearing.* Someone with a lot of food and wine knowledge selects what wine to serve with each course. It's supposed to enhance the meal. You know, a different wine paired with each dish."

She looked around, wide-eyed as the head chef, as instructed, served us course after course at our little table in the corner of the kitchen. We were out of the way but could still see and hear most of what was going on.

Bel leaned toward me like she had a secret. "This is the coolest thing ever. I love cooking, too. I mean, I haven't done anything fancy, but I cooked for my aunt and sister whenever I could when I was growing up."

"What did you cook?"

She dabbed her mouth. "Well, basic stuff, but I did roast a chicken once."

"How'd it come out?"

She laughed. "A little dry. But everyone pretended that they loved it. And I learned to cook it ten minutes less the next time."

She was transformed, nearly glowing from the inside, talking about happier days. The burden of her current situation, being stalked by a loser ex, had exited her thoughts, at least for a moment.

And I loved it.

"Oh my god," she said, patting her stomach. "This has been incredible. I'm not sure I can eat any more."

I was surprised she'd eaten as much as she had. But glad.

I finished my wine. "Let's get out of here then."

She had one last sip of her wine, leaving the glass half full like she did all the other pairings we'd been served. "There's no bill to pay? Nothing?"

"Sweetie, I told you we own the restaurants in the hotel. Of course we get free meals. Within reason. If I came down here every night of the week, someone would say something. But once in a while is expected."

"Okay, then. Let's go," she said gamely.

21

SAMUELE "SAMMY" CAPUTO

"ARE YOU COLD, BEL?"

She nodded, rubbing her bare arms as we walked through the casino toward the elevators. I slipped my suit jacket off and draped it around her shoulders.

"I never realized how chilly it is in here. I guess I'm usually wearing something covering my arms," she said.

I scanned the slots like I did every time I walked through. Force of habit. "We keep it cool so people don't get tired."

"I suppose if people are alert they'll keep gambling?"

She was catching on.

I slung an arm around her shoulder. "That's the idea."

As we walked, she leaned into me. I couldn't help but smile.

Bingo.

And when we reached the elevator, I leaned down to kiss her again. This time, unlike the night before in the bar, she wasn't surprised. In fact, she seemed ready for me. She put her hands on either side of my face and let her eyes fall closed.

I, of course, kept mine open. I wanted to never stop looking at her.

Once we were in the elevator, I backed her against the mirrored walls and kissed her even harder. We had cameras in all our elevators, and I was pretty sure the security guys were enjoying my show. I didn't care, and I didn't stop until the doors opened.

I took Bel's key card and inserted it into the door, but when I pushed it open and let her enter, I didn't follow. I wanted to, but I didn't. I knew to take my time with this woman.

She leaned against the doorjamb. "I have to tell you something, Sammy."

I twirled a piece of her hair between my fingers. "Yeah?"

"I kissed Dom the other day. Before you."

I pressed my lips to her temple. It was not easy to stay out of her room, and my dick was throbbing.

"I know that."

She jerked back. "You know? You're not mad?"

Her integrity was charming.

I shook my head, no. "It's okay. Totally okay. In fact, you can kiss Tristan too, if you haven't already."

She tilted her head. "Seriously?"

"Uh-huh. It's a thing with us. We're cool with sharing as long as it's limited to the three of us."

The look on her face, with her wide eyes and parted lips, told me she was processing what I'd said. She was confused. And surprised.

Everyone was, at first.

And now was not the time to elaborate. I had to get the hell out of there before I pushed my way in and stayed until morning.

I stepped back out of the doorway and into the hall. "Thank you for joining me. I'm glad you enjoyed your first chef's table."

She looked confused that I was leaving. Which was good. Keep her guessing.

I turned and headed back to the elevator.

Pure torture.

"WHAT ARE YOU IDIOTS UP TO?"

"Watching the game, what's it look like?" Dom said, not looking away from the TV.

I tossed my jacket on the back of one of three sofas in the living room of the penthouse I shared with the guys. Tristan and Dom were sprawled on the other two, one in workout clothes, the other in PJ bottoms. I kicked off my own shoes and put my feet up on the coffee table.

Tristan was not as invested in the game and turned to me. "Hey. How was dinner? You did the chef's table, right?"

He might be trying to play it cool, but his face was hopeful, just as I'd expected it to be. I knew he liked Bel and was eager to see if she might be into our unique sort of arrangement.

"It was great. I really enjoyed myself and she did, too. You should have seen her, man, with that pale skin in that black dress I got her. She was turning heads everywhere she went."

"Nice."

"So, you like her, Tristan?" I asked.

He nodded. "Yup."

That made three of us, then.

"She told me she'd kissed Dom. Like it was a bad thing. I told her it was fine and to go ahead and kiss you, too."

Tristan dropped his head back and laughed. "Did her head spin?"

"A little. You know how it is when they first find out that we share. But I kissed her goodnight and left her to think about it."

Dom finally tore himself from the game and joined the conversation. "What? What did I miss?"

"Sammy had a good time with Bel," Tristan said. "Now I have to see if I can get a bit of time with her."

"Does she know anything about our arrangement?" Dom asked.

Grabbing my jacket and shoes, I stood. I was exhausted, and dying for a hot shower where I could jerk off. "I made reference to it but did not elaborate. It's too soon."

Dom nodded.

I scanned the massive penthouse apartment we'd had designed for the three of us. People might think it strange that three grown men more or less lived together, but those would be people who didn't know us.

We each had a suite consisting of a bedroom and office, and of course a private bathroom. We could hang out in the living room and watch games or whatever, or in the kitchen to cook and eat, but we could also retreat into our places for privacy. And we had entrances direct to the hallway. We didn't have to go through the common space if we didn't want to.

The best part was we also had a fourth room for a... special friend. It was currently empty.

That's where Bel came in. Or we hoped would come in.

"Sounds like we're in agreement on moving things forward. If she's on board."

Dom looked happy for a change. "You know I don't usually like to do this with people we work with, but I think an exception is called for. Someone like Bel does not come along every day. She can even quit her job. She doesn't need the money if she's with us."

"I bet she keeps working," Tristan said.

If she agreed to our arrangement, she'd be with the three richest men in Las Vegas. She'd never have to work another day in her life. There might be dangers, like Damian coveting her, but we could handle shit like that.

And I thought Tristan was probably right. She'd keep working. It's just the way she was.

22

ANNABEL "BEL" SIMMONS

In what world was a guy okay with kissing you when his friend had just the day before?

These Vegas guys were weird, and I was still trying to wrap my head around what Sammy had said.

"It's a thing with us. We're cool with sharing as long as it's limited to the three of us."

What in the hell did that mean?

But I'd figure that out later. In the meantime, my feet were screaming in pain from the heels I'd worn all night. I kicked them off and was heading for the bathroom to soak in the tub when I noticed a shopping bag next to my door that I hadn't seen before.

It was made of thick, heavy paper covered in fancy

embossing. The handles were sturdy grosgrain ribbon, clipped together for easier carrying.

Someone had been shopping, and it hadn't been at Target. The bag was so pretty it seemed like it ought to be on display.

Stilettos in hand, I brought the bag to the sofa and started sifting through it.

The first thing I pulled out was a note. *"We wanted to make sure you were comfortable in your new place. Dom, Sammy, & Tristan."*

Inside the bag were garments, each carefully wrapped in tissue paper. I started with the largest one, and as the tissue paper fell away, I ran my hands over what was possibly the softest thing I'd ever felt. I shook it out to find it was a long, cashmere robe the color of sand. The label said 'Carine Gilson.' I'd never heard of her but she must make some amazing things. I mean, a robe made from cashmere? That was the epitome of extravagance.

I ran to the bathroom and held it up to myself in front of the long mirror. It was delicious, like a cupcake that's too perfect to eat. I slipped out of my dress and wrapped the gorgeous, slinky knit around my body, cinching it with a tie belt.

Turning up the collar at the back of my neck, I pulled it snug. It just brushed the tops of my feet and when I walked, it swayed heavily. I felt like I was wrapped in a dozen warm, protective hands. I closed my eyes and rubbed the collar against my face.

Oh. My. God.

I didn't think I would ever take it off, but then I remembered the rest of the bag. I ran back to the sofa.

It couldn't get any better than this, but I sure wanted to see if the guys had tried.

The next thing I pulled out of the bag was a set of PJs, same color as the robe, but made of silk. There was a delicate drawstring on the pants, and the top was trimmed in covered buttons. They were so incredibly fine. Too fine to sleep in.

Maybe I could just hang them in my closet and look at them every now and then? The thought of tossing, turning, snoring, and occasionally drooling while wearing this stuff seemed like a travesty.

The entire set probably cost more than I earned in a week. Actually, a month.

After that, I opened a long nightgown of the same silk as the PJ set, also from Carine Gilson. I ran my fingers over the soft silk. It was amazing, but when would I ever wear it?

The last thing in the bag was wrapped in a different color tissue paper. I shook out yet another PJ set, this one in the softest white cotton, from Frette. Obviously, another fancy brand.

I spread out my new goodies over the sofa and looked at them one by one, lovingly stroking them and imagining wearing them around my suite like a lady of leisure.

I'd be lying if I didn't also admit I imagined wearing

them for the guys. And after Sammy's mysterious comment, I wondered if maybe I'd have the chance.

Oh, hell.

Taking off the robe, I threw it on the sofa with the other gifts and headed to the bathroom to soak, berating myself for even thinking there was a world where one woman could be with three guys.

The fact was, I couldn't be with *any* of them. I *worked* for them.

But they were so amazing to me. I'd never been treated like a princess, and while I wouldn't want it all the time, it sure as hell was amazing when it happened.

I thought of my sister as I sank into my warm, bubbly bath. Would it be rude to send her one of the PJ sets the guys had gotten me? I knew she'd never had anything that nice, just like I hadn't. I wanted to share my good fortune with her. But there would be questions. Lots of questions. Maggie was no dummy. She'd go right to Google to find out how much everything cost. And she'd want to know who the hell had given it to me.

I wasn't ready to share that with her, or with anyone for that matter. Maybe I never would. This was just a quick bleep on the long screen of my life. I would savor it as long as it lasted because there was no freaking way it was permanent.

But the guys did like me. At least it seemed like it. And they weren't being nice just to get laid. The way Sammy had dropped me off at my door after dinner with no expectation was the most gentlemanly thing I'd ever seen. But it also left me aching.

Actually, everything about the guys left me aching.

Which was not good.

So while I appreciated that they hadn't pushed themselves on me, it was probably best to curtail their… courting, if that's what it was, before things got hot and heavy. And hell, they were also involved in some sort of crime syndicate thing with guns and god knew what else. I didn't need that kind of complicated shit in my life. I was trying to get it together, not attract more trouble.

I needed to keep my job, keep my head down, and keep saving money.

Speaking of Maggie, I'd left a bracelet she'd given me at the motel when I'd run out on Len. It wasn't anything particularly valuable, but it was the only thing I had from a family member, and I knew she must have scraped the money together to buy it for me. I wondered if Kate might be able to get it for me. I'd run over there myself, but if the guys found out, they'd go insane.

I supposed if the bracelet was all I lost during this craziness, maybe I had nothing to complain about.

"You look amazing, Bel."

Thank god the lighting was dim in the nightclub the

guys had taken me to, because my face was heating up. It would be only moments before it was bright red.

"Thank you, Tristan."

I had to admit, I felt pretty goddamn sexy. Among the many pieces of clothing the guys got me was a gorgeous pair of black silk, wide-legged trousers. I topped it off with a silver sequined halter-top just wide enough to cover my boobs, secured by thin straps tied behind my neck and back. Strappy heels and glittery earrings topped it off.

I looked over the private room's balcony to the floor below where people were dancing to booming house music.

Of course the guys had gotten a private room. Everything they did was first class. It was just how they rolled. It didn't matter that we were in the most exclusive Vegas nightclub. Nothing was out of their reach. Even the champagne the impossibly beautiful waitress had just poured was the best.

Dom Perignon. I'd seen it on the menus of the places I'd eaten with the guys.

It was crazy expensive.

And after my first sip, I could see why. The bubbles were super fine, and the flavor was a perfect balance of sweet land dry.

Dom and Sammy sat back on a leather sofa, relaxing with their legs crossed that way that guys do, each sipping some sort of amber liquor.

Tristan sat on the edge of his own chair, rocking his

head in time to the music and drinking beer from a bottle.

They were masters of the universe, all three of them. Even if their universe revolved around illegal shit.

"Bel, why don't you come over here and sit down? We'd like to talk to you."

Dom patted his hand on the sofa between Sammy and himself.

Aware that all eyes were on me, I sauntered over and took a seat. The evening was just getting going and I hadn't felt so happy and at ease since... well, I couldn't say.

Tristan stopped moving to the music, his face serious.

Oh no. Were they firing me? Kicking me out of my suite?

The evening's magic began to slip away. I desperately wanted to hang on to it, but when I thought about how precarious my existence was and how dependent I was on the guys, I remembered that I should never get too comfortable. I needed to be on my guard at all times, ready for the worst.

I took a deep breath and braced myself. "Yes? What was it you wanted to talk about?" I croaked.

I finished my champagne. It might be a long time before I had another like it.

Sammy took one of my hands, intertwining our

fingers. His skin was soft and warm, but I still didn't let myself get too comfortable.

"We'd like for you to be with us, like I mentioned to you the other night."

Relief washed over me. I wasn't getting fired, dumped, or kicked out. Yet.

And I'd been wondering when I might hear more about the sharing thing he'd brought up. But I'd been hesitant to ask.

Dom looked at me, his gaze as intense as always. If I didn't know he liked me, I'd swear he hated me.

It's just how he was.

Unlike Tristan, who wore his heart on his sleeve. He was the sweetest of the three, and yet the only one I'd not kissed. Yet.

And Sammy. My savior. Of course, I could have saved myself. I eventually would have. But he taught me I was worth saving and why.

"I... I'm not sure what that means—for me to be with you."

Tristan stepped in. "You've probably figured out by now that we're... different from most guys you've known."

Different was right—they were perfect specimens of human maleness. Like the universe had been in a very good mood the day it created them.

Dom smiled at me, something he rarely did, and the crinkles around his eyes just about melted my panties. "You've learned about our business dealings, both the above board and not-so-above board. We don't share that with just anyone. You are special to us, Bel. We'd like to date you. All three of us."

I looked at each of them, one at a time, to make sure they were serious. If they weren't, it was a shitty joke.

"Date all three of you. I'm not sure what that means or how it would work. But it sounds… interesting."

Actually, it sounded hot as hell. But I didn't want to seem too enthusiastic.

And why the hell not? It could be weird working with the guys and dating them, whatever that meant, but I could try it for as long as it lasted. Everyone else in Vegas was having fun. Why not me?

If things blew up, I always had that cash in the lining of my purse. And I had more in the bank, since I'd gotten my first paycheck.

Dom got to his feet. "*Interesting*, she says, boys." He looked at the others.

"I'll take *interesting*," Sammy said, bringing me to my feet.

"Where… where are we going?"

Tristan leaned over and kissed my temple. "We have something to show you."

He took my hand and we headed downstairs, with Dom and Sammy right behind us.

"Wait. We're leaving? But we just got here," I said, holding Tristan's hand as we crossed the club and left via a different door than the one we'd entered through.

"Don't worry, baby. We'll be back another night."

23

ANNABEL "BEL" SIMMONS

"Wow. What is this place?"

"This, my beautiful, is our home. And your home now, too. If you want it to be."

I turned to take it all in. It was similar to my suite in some ways with the same lighting and floors, but it was decorated with a stronger, masculine sort of feel. Which I guess made sense. And it was massive, several times larger than my suite. In fact, from where I stood, I couldn't see where it ended.

"You guys… live together?"

Tristan laughed and took my hand. "That's everybody's first question. We each have our own suite, and the living room we're standing in right now is shared. Our penthouse has the entire top floor of the hotel."

Holy shit. It was larger than most free-standing homes.

No wonder I couldn't see where it ended—because it basically didn't.

"My god. You have the entire floor."

He nodded. "Yup. Dom's place is over there, this one is mine, and the one on the other side is Sammy's."

I pointed toward the one remaining apartment, which I could see through its partially open door. "What's that one?"

Sammy clapped his hands. "That's what we wanted to show you. C'mon."

We passed through a sort of sitting room or office with overstuffed white furniture and a huge armoire, probably holding a TV, to the biggest bedroom I'd ever seen in my life.

Which really wasn't saying much. But still.

A massive four-poster bed was the main attraction. It was draped in crushed velvet and covered in throw pillows. I turned to find a chaise in one corner and— holy shit—a fireplace.

Long, heavy draperies framed the windows, and there were fresh flowers on nearly every flat surface. I passed a giant fiddle leaf fig on my way to peek into a closet larger than any place I'd ever lived.

And it was full of clothes.

"This is for you. All of it."

I turned in a circle to take it in again. "This is so weird, but this room is exactly my taste."

My taste if I could have anything I wanted, that was.

"We know that. It was designed just for you."

I whipped around to face Sammy. "What? What do you mean?"

He shrugged. "We have people who do research on... other people. Do you have Pinterest? That's where they probably figured out what you like."

They stalked my Pinterest?

"You had this place decorated just for me? But I have my own suite that I'm staying in, downstairs."

When they looked at each other, I realized my life was changing.

First, I had no idea these guys lived so lavishly. And then, they'd decorated a room just for me, even though I already had a perfectly good suite a few floors below?

Dom walked over to an enormous dresser. "We were hoping, Bel, that you'd want to be with us, even if just for a trial basis." He slid the top drawer open and pulled out a slim, black box.

"And if you're open to our arrangement, we have a gift for you," he said, handing it to me.

I accepted the box but just stood there, unsure what to do.

"Open it," he said.

I slipped the top off. Inside was a shiny gold necklace. Actually, it was more of a choker. It reminded me of a bangle bracelet, but it was big enough for a neck. It was simple with clean lines, but also luxurious. And heavy.

I could only imagine how much it must have cost. Gold was expensive and I knew these guys didn't buy fakes.

In addition to the necklace, the box also held a tiny key. I picked it up and twirled it in my fingers when it dawned on me that the key was for the necklace. Which locked.

Strange. Why would a necklace need a lock?

"Look inside it, Bel," Dom said, nodding.

The necklace was engraved with the guys' initials: *D. S. T.*

"As long as you are with us, you will wear this. It will remind you at all times that you are ours. It can always be removed at your request, but then our arrangement will end."

Sammy walked over to me and took the necklace. He slipped it around my neck and took the key out of my other hand. There was a little twisting grind of metal, and he turned me by the shoulders to face him and admire his handiwork. He dropped the key into his pocket.

"We all have a copy of the key, so don't worry."

My hands flew to the cold metal, rapidly warming against my skin. It was hard to the touch but strangely comforting in its solidity. I tugged at it as a test, and ran my fingers over the lock.

It was not coming off, at least not by my hand.

I kept stroking it. I liked it. "All my stuff is downstairs. In my suite."

Tristan waved a hand as if to say *don't worry*. "We'll have it brought up tomorrow morning. In the meantime, there are PJs in that dresser over there, and the closet is full of new clothes your size. Not that you have to worry about what to wear since tomorrow is Saturday, after all. You can sleep in or do whatever you want."

"But, but, but…"

He walked over and gave me the sweetest kiss on the cheek. "You'll live with us now, at least until the arrangement ends by your choice or ours. You can walk at any time, no hard feelings. You can keep working for us for as long as you want, too, but you don't have to. We will support you in any way that we can, always. But of course, we hope you'll be happy. And stay."

They moved to leave me and after a flurry of *good-nights*, pulled my door shut.

Okay. What the hell had just happened?

First, the guys wanted to date me. How did that work?

Then, they put a necklace on me that only they could take off. Heart pounding, I ran to the mirror to check it out. It was actually completely normal looking. No one would know I couldn't remove it on my own.

But what did it mean? And why did it require a key

to remove it? Was it some sort of kinky ownership thing?

Because if it was, I was turned on as hell.

Maybe I should have been repulsed by the idea of the guys owning me.

But I wasn't. So fuck that.

And last, I had yet another new place to live, even though my suite had been perfectly fine. In fact, I'd gotten very comfortable in it. But they wanted me close by.

I took off my nightclub clothes and pulled on my new PJs. Once in bed, I pulled the fluffy down comforter up to my neck. I hoped there wouldn't be any more surprises for a while.

I'd had enough to last for a long time.

24

TRISTANO "TRISTAN" LASTRA

"W̲h̲a̲t̲ ̲a̲r̲e̲ ̲y̲o̲u̲ ̲d̲o̲i̲n̲g̲, Tris? Not coming to the gym?"

The guys were in their workout clothes, heading out, with Dom in a pulled-up hoodie and Sammy in a ratty Pink Floyd T-shirt, his hair in a ponytail. I usually went to the gym with them. But not today.

Which raised instant suspicion. Sometimes I wished I just lived alone—like completely alone—where I never had to deal with anyone until I was good and ready to.

But the advantages of living with the guys were many, and usually outweighed the small irritations.

"I'm chilling," I said, not looking up from the newspaper I was reading. I flipped to the business section and pretended the guys weren't there.

But I knew what was coming.

"You're waiting for her, aren't you?" Sammy sang.

"No, dude, I'm reading the fucking newspaper."

I finally looked up and caught the guys looking at each other, smirks all over their faces.

I closed the paper and reached for my coffee. But I was so irritated, I spilled half of it on my PJ bottoms.

Goddammit. Those were expensive.

"Hey, no need to get your panties in a twist," Dom laughed.

They left for their workouts.

I loved those guys. They were my friends. But sometimes a man just doesn't want anyone in his business.

Like right now.

I was tired, which meant I was cranky. And the guys knew just how to push my buttons.

Fuck if I wasn't up half the night thinking about Bel, just a few yards away under my own roof.

To try and remedy the situation, I'd jerked off multiple times. I finally had to stop because I was getting sore. That hadn't happened since I was a teenager. But with Bel so close I might as well have been a teenager again, desperate to get laid. It was all I could fucking think about.

We'd had women join our 'special arrangement'

before, and move into the Penthouse, but I didn't remember ever craving someone as badly as I did Bel.

Well, she hadn't technically moved in. Her things were supposed to be delivered at any moment. I guess at that point, she'd be formally 'moved in.' She could bail anytime she wanted to.

But she wouldn't. I knew she wouldn't. We were offering her something she'd never had before. She was smart enough to see that.

And it started with respect.

I'm not saying we guys were perfect. Far from it. Shit, we earned our living doing questionably legal things. But we saw something in Bel, and we could give her what she needed.

That she was stunning and sexy was icing on the cake.

Personally, if she walked away today knowing she deserved better than the creep she'd been with, I'd feel like I'd done a good thing.

'Course I hoped she'd stick around longer than that.

And like the guys had said, before they'd left for the gym and gotten out of my damn face, I was indeed waiting for her to get her ass out of bed. Yup, right here on the sofa in the living room, facing her door, so the minute she came out, I'd see her.

Nobody knew it, but I hadn't exactly spent the entire night in my own room. I'd slipped into Bel's and watched her while she slept, all angelic and shit and making the occasional girl snore. If she found out, she'd definitely think I was a freak. She'd be right.

Especially if she knew I'd grabbed a pair of her panties off the floor and put them to good use.

Yeah, she'd never see those again. They were covered in my cum. And boy, did I enjoy myself imagining her wearing those things. And covering them with more cum.

I'd hoped when I left her room and got back in my own bed, sleep would come easily. But I laid awake another couple hours.

And now, here I was, awake in an overtired, jetlagged sort of way, staring at her closed door.

As if I could will it to open. And don't you know, that's exactly when her bedroom door flew open, just as I was adjusting myself. I pulled the newspaper over my lap and smiled innocently.

"Well, if it isn't sleeping beauty."

She pulled the plushy robe I'd left in her room more tightly around herself and yawned while she worked her way to the living room.

"Morning Tristan. What time is it?" she asked, yawning.

Damn she was cute, wearing a too-big robe, her wild hair framing her head like a halo.

She caught me staring and tried to smooth down the curls. "I must look a mess, sorry."

"It's early. And no need to apologize. I'm not exactly

presentable myself." I pointed to my coffee-stained PJ bottoms.

She curled up in a chair opposite me, tucking her legs under her slim body. "Wow. I slept so well. There's something about that room. I was so comfortable... like a sanctuary. Or a womb."

I was glad to hear that. Very glad.

The door bell rang and I jumped to get it.

"Who's that?" she asked.

"You'll see."

I pulled open the door and accepted a large grocery bag from my bellman friend. He poked his head in and waved. "Hi, Miss Simmons."

She craned her neck to see. "Hello Jim."

I slipped him a fifty like I always did. Guaranteed good service. Discreet, too.

He entered the room quietly, pulling a large garment rack and bags full of Bel's things from downstairs.

"Oh. Let me help with that." She jumped up.

But I put my hands up. "He's got it, Bel. He'll unpack for you."

Surprise crossed her face and she turned her attention to the grocery bag. "What's all this? It smells awesome."

I began pulling things out of the bag. "This is McDonald's breakfast."

Her eyes widened and she grinned. Exactly the reaction I'd been hoping for. "Oh my god. My favorite."

I already knew that. Emails, you know.

She lunged for an Egg McMuffin and sank her teeth into it, closing her eyes and moaning. "I know this is horrible junk food. But it's so yummy. And comforting."

I grabbed one for myself. I couldn't lie. I loved a good McDonald's breakfast from time to time.

After she'd inhaled her first, she grabbed a plain biscuit and slathered it with butter and jelly.

A woman after my own heart.

"I'll tell ya, Tristan. You really know how to treat a girl." She dropped her head back and belted out a lovely unselfconscious laugh.

"We can go somewhere nice, later, if you want."

The last bite of biscuit disappeared into her mouth. "Oh my god, I love this. Believe me, I wasn't complaining."

The bellman emerged from her room without a sound and disappeared out the door with his empty rack.

She then dove for one of those semi-frozen orange juices in the plastic cup, the kind with the peel-off foil top, swallowing it down in one gulp.

"Oh my god. That was so good." She rubbed her belly.

"Okay. I'll tell you what. Why don't you get dressed and we'll go out. I want to take you shopping."

A smile crept across her face. I was ready for what she would say next.

"Oh. You don't have to do that. You've gotten me so many things already."

I gestured toward her room with my chin. "Go. Get dressed. We're going."

Her eyebrows rose and she hesitated. But then she jumped up and beelined for her room, pulling the door closed behind her.

I went into my own room to get out of my stained PJ bottoms, and pulled on a pair of jeans and a sports jacket. The guys loved to give me shit, but I liked dressing nicely, even if it was the weekend. Shit, I was the only one out of the three of us who wore a suit every day. Dom had a kind of motorcycle club thing going on with the leather jacket he wore, and Sammy was our resident rocker with his beat up old T-shirts and ponytail. One of us had to dress like a grown up.

No, we weren't your typical syndicate guys. We were the new generation, and did things differently.

When I returned to the living room, I found Bel had beaten me there. The excitement on her face gave away her enthusiasm and she jumped to her feet.

Wearing skinny jeans with holes in the knees and Keds sneakers.

With a closet full of expensive, designer clothes just feet away.

But that was okay. She was being herself.

"Ready?" I asked, taking her hand.

"Absolutely."

She gripped my fingers right back.

25

TRISTANO "TRISTAN" LASTRA

Because it was Saturday, the hotel—and really everything in Vegas—was teeming with crowds.

You had your rowdy bachelor and bachelorette parties, eloping couples, soccer moms on their girls' weekend away, conventioneers wearing big name badges, and people who'd met for a clandestine weekend away. This town had something for everyone.

The cross section of humanity that visited Vegas was mind blowing.

And that's what I loved about it.

"Here we go," I said, leading Bel out of the throngs and into a high-end lingerie store in the hotel's elegant shopping court.

187

She regarded the place with wide eyes. "Oh my god. This stuff is amazing. Is this where you got the other things you gave me?"

"It's one of the places."

I waved over to the store manager, who I knew well. She, like the bellman, was another trusted and discreet employee.

They were hard to come by, so we paid them well.

"Mr. Lastra," she cooed.

Yeah. I'd fucked her. In fact, I'd thought briefly about bringing her to the guys to see if she was a fit for our arrangement. But she was a high maintenance pain in the ass. And she didn't like giving head.

She rubbed her fake tits on me when Bel wandered away through the store, touching everything she saw like it was gold.

"When are we getting together again?" she pouted.

I took a deep breath. "We're not, Nadia. I'm sorry."

I didn't like to be a dick. But sometimes a guy just has to.

She wasn't deterred. "Well, you know where to find me if you should change your mind." She glanced over at Bel, who was in awe of some panties likely made of some of the world's finest lace.

"She's pretty. I don't blame you."

She was a good sport as well as good at her job. "Can you pick out some things for her? Put them in a dressing room?"

She nodded and approached Bel.

I had no freaking idea what our lovely girl liked. Hell, she probably didn't know, either. She doubtless got her underwear at Target or the GAP for all I knew. But those days were behind her now. She might not yet fully grasp the privilege of being part of our arrangement, but she would soon.

And I knew she'd always be humble about it.

Bel came over to me, exploding with delight. "Nadia's putting a bunch of stuff in the fitting room for me. I couldn't choose. Everything was so beautiful. So I asked her to decide."

Nadia waved from the dressing room. "We're ready for you, dear."

Bel scurried to check out her new treasures.

I took a seat in the area where the husbands and sugar daddies waited, and flipped through a back issue of *Town and Country*. I watched Bel's bare feet below the dressing room door and each time she let another lacy thing pool around her feet, my dick got a little harder.

Finally, I couldn't wait any longer.

I approached the door and knocked lightly. "Bel? How's it going?"

"Oh my god, I don't know how I'll choose."

"How about if I help you?" I asked through the door. "Let me in."

The door opened slowly and she peeked out.

"No need to hide, baby. They can't kick us out."

She pushed the door the rest of the way open and when I was inside, pulled it shut behind me.

Holy shit. She was wearing a tiny string panty and matching bra that pushed up her small tits *just so*. The fabric was a sheer sort of netting with little pink and yellow flowers embroidered all over.

Sweet and sexy all at the same time. Not everyone could pull that off.

I made myself comfortable on the bench in the corner. I was going to enjoy this. "Turn around."

She looked at me shyly at first, then slowly rotated until I could see the firm flesh of her ass, accented by the straps of her thong, just like a frame around a beautiful painting.

Fuck me.

When she faced me again, I nodded. "Very nice. We'll take those two pieces."

Emboldened, she struck a pose, hands on hips. "Shall I try another set?"

Was she fucking kidding?

"Yup. Waiting."

She slowly reached behind her back and unclasped the bra, letting the delicate garment float to the floor. And there were her lovely little tits, full on the bottom with pale, upturned nipples that jiggled the tiniest bit when she moved.

She hooked her thumbs on the strings of her thong, lowering it down her hips one side at a time, drawing out her naughty tease while my gaze moved between her big eyes and her lovely body.

But when the thong was down far enough, I was able to feast my eyes on her pretty, shaved pussy.

Okay, there was no hiding my hard on now. I shifted it in my pants until I was able relieve some of the discomfort.

"C'mere," I growled. "And put your foot here." I pointed to the arm of the chair where I was sitting.

She lifted her leg, placing her foot exactly where I'd instructed, and as a result opened her sex for me to see.

Her pussy was beautiful, pink, and glistening, and when I lightly touched her lips I saw the white cream that told me I had our girl turned on.

"Sweet," I murmured, leaning in for a taste.

Bel placed one hand on the wall and the other on my head for balance and rocked into my mouth. Almost immediately, her legs began to quiver, and her breath turned into short gasps.

I withdrew my tongue to run my thumb over her hard clit, all the time watching her, eyes closed, wearing the slightest hint of a smile. Other customers milled around outside the dressing room with no clue of what was going on this side of our door.

Nearly drove me out of my mind.

"Baby," I whispered.

Her eyes fluttered open.

"I want you to come in my mouth."

She grabbed my head with her two hands, grinding

herself right into my face like the greedy little thing she was.

Holy fuck.

I pulled her to me with one hand on her ass, and grabbed her tit with my other.

"Oh… oh… Tristan…" she whispered hoarsely.

"C'mon, baby."

She shuddered with a climax. Her legs gave out and I caught her just in time, pulling her to my lap and pressing my lips to hers.

"You like the way you taste?" I asked, pulling back.

"Yeah."

I nodded toward the garments she'd not tried on yet. "You have some other things to model for me."

She sighed, nuzzling into my neck. "I don't know. I'm kind of worn out."

No problem.

"That's fine. We'll just buy everything, then."

26

ANNABEL "BEL" SIMMONS

"Who is it?"

I bolted upright in bed, yanking the covers to my neck, to find Sammy wheeling a cart into my room.

He pushed it to the side of the bed opposite where I was, propped up a pillow for himself, and hopped in. "It's me, Sammy. I wanted to surprise you."

"You *did* surprise me when you banged the cart through my door."

He grabbed the TV remote and started clicking at the giant wall-mounted screen opposite my bed as the breakfast smells from the cart made their way to me.

"Oh, yeah. That cart is unwieldy. Good thing I'm

not a bellman." He laughed and settled on an old episode of *Three Stooges*.

The Three Stooges?

Was I awake or dreaming in some sort of weird alternate universe where a rock 'n roll hottie and organized crime guy watched slapstick comedy?

Further unnerving were his plaid PJ bottoms and bare chest. As he shifted around on my bed getting comfortable, his muscles rippled just enough to remind me they were there. And were very nice-looking.

I wouldn't have minded running my fingers over them, but I still had the comforter pulled up to my chin with both hands, wondering if I needed to start locking my bedroom door at night.

I finally had my first view of his sleeve tattoos. Finely detailed, they were dark and kind of goth. I didn't know much about tattoos, but I knew it was expensive to get good ones.

And those ones looked pretty good.

"How'd you sleep?" he asked.

Since we were going to pretend this was normal, I figured I might as well go along.

Cute guy barges into my room with a fancy breakfast on a cart, turns on the Three Stooges, and makes himself at home in my bed.

But when I thought about it, what about my life *was* normal?

I worked for three guys involved in organized crime who'd moved me out of a shitty motel where I'd lived with a boyfriend, to a fancy penthouse. They bought me clothes the likes of which I never even knew existed and if that weren't enough, wanted to *share* me.

Oh, and I'd messed around with one of them in a lingerie shop dressing room.

So if any of that was normal, I'd sure like to know what wasn't.

"Mimosa?" Sammy asked, pushing his too-long hair back and handing me a champagne glass.

I took a big swallow. I'd only had a mimosa once before and I remembered thinking it was about the best thing I'd ever tasted. What was it about orange juice mixed with champagne?

As the sweet, bubbly liquid reached my stomach, I relaxed. A calming warmth washed over me and I propped up my pillows just like Sammy so I could see the TV, too.

Might as well join the party.

I peeked over at the cart. "What else you got there?"

"All kinds of good stuff," he said, handing me his glass.

He grabbed a small plate and put the largest scone I'd ever seen on it. "Here you go. Blueberry."

Oh my god. I was sitting in bed with a gorgeous, shirtless man, drinking mimosas, and he'd just handed me a blueberry scone.

My favorite food group.

"How did you know?" I asked, stuffing the corner into my mouth like a starved animal.

"How did I know what? That you love blueberry scones? Bel, we guys know shit. We pay attention. And then take action."

I didn't know whether to be tickled or afraid.

But Sammy just looked so good there, sitting in my bed and feeding me, that I didn't worry for long.

"Do you like blueberry scones too?"

He glanced over at the cart. "Yeah. I do. But they only brought us one. Bastards."

"I could share mine. If you like."

The corner of his mouth turned up. "That would be most kind of you. I really, really would like a taste of some of that blueberry magic."

I broke off a corner of the scone and offered it to him. But instead of letting him take it in his fingers, I aimed for his mouth.

Yeah, I felt like having some fun.

I pushed the crumbly pastry past his slightly parted lips, and he devoured it.

"Mmmm," he moaned, closing his eyes. "That is a damn good blueberry scone."

I scooted closer and brought my champagne flute to his lips. "Here's a little something to help wash it down."

With his gaze on mine, he tilted his head for a sip.

But just as it reached his lips, I tipped the glass a little too far, letting several drops run down his bare chest.

"Oh no. Look at the mess I made. Poor Sammy," I teased.

He fake-grimaced. "Yeah. I'm just a mess."

He reached for a napkin, but I stopped him.

"Let me. It's the least I can do since I… got you all dirty." I scooted over to his side of the bed and straddled him.

His hands on my thighs, he looked up at me. "You got me wet, baby."

I ran a finger along his lower lip to brush away one last crumb of scone, and leaned down to lick the spilled mimosa off his chest.

His skin was smooth, smelling of fresh, sage-y soap and of course orange juice and champagne. After I'd cleansed him of my spill, I peeked up to find him watching me, wearing a satisfied smile. I returned my lips to his chest, at first covering his dark nipples with small kisses, then trailing them to his stomach.

It didn't take long for a tent to appear in his PJ pants, and while I was itching to get my hands on the culprit, I held off. If he hadn't gotten a hard on as fast as he did, it would have been my personal mission to give him one.

And because I'd managed to kiss and lick my way down his chest to the waistband of his PJs, there was only one thing left to do.

"These are kind of in my way," I said, gesturing at his PJ bottoms.

He nodded gravely. "I can see that."

"I may have to remove them."

He nodded again, all serious. "I think you should."

I scooted off his lap until I was over his knees and slipped his PJ bottoms below his ass, catching his erection in their waistband, and watching it bounce back against his belly button.

And what an erection it was. Long, and smooth, with the sort of thickness every girl dreams of. The head was big and round, glistening with a smear of precum.

There was no turning back now, even if in the back of my mind was the useless, annoying reminder that on Monday, I'd have to face this guy in the office.

Fuck that. It was still Sunday.

Sammy watched, wondering what I'd do with my first meeting of his hard cock. He didn't need to wait long.

I grasped it, my fingers barely closing, and licked the precum off his head.

His breath caught from the sensation. He leaned back, putting his hands behind his head as he spread his legs so I could kneel between them.

"That's nice, baby," he said in a raspy voice.

I smoothed a hand up his abdomen and over his chest, absorbing his radiating heat. I was dying to throw my little nightgown aside to cool down, but I didn't want to give away how wet I was. I got a whiff of my excitement and it would only be a matter of time before Sammy did, too.

Perspiration broke out on my brow while I glided my lips down the shaft of Sammy's cock, stopping only when it bounced against the back of my throat. With my free left hand I gripped him at the root and stroked what I couldn't get in my mouth, matching the rhythm of my bobbing head.

"Fuck baby," he groaned. "Slow down. I don't want to come."

I never understood why guys said that. Just *come*.

And then get hard again.

Sammy placed on hand on my head to control my speed, gently pushing me up and down while playing with my locked collar. Then, with a swift motion, he took me by the shoulders and pushed me off.

It was so unexpected that my mouth hung open as if he were still inside it, and saliva dripped down my chin.

"Stand over there and get undressed," he growled in a voice I hadn't heard before.

And that voice owned me. He could have told me to jump out the penthouse window and I probably would have. I would do whatever he wanted. I didn't know why. I just knew I would.

He nodded at the window. "Open the blinds."

I let the bright sun into the room while he reached into the nightstand next to my bed and retrieved a condom.

Presumptuous? Yes.

But I wasn't about to argue. If they stashed condoms in my nightstand, I was good with that.

He got to his feet, kicking aside his PJs.

I drew my nightie over my head, now naked in front of a window overlooking a vast expanse of Vegas.

"Face it."

I pointed. "What? Face the window?"

He nodded.

"Now, put your hands on it and step away until you are bent at a ninety-degree angle."

Holy shit. He was going to see all my goodies.

I obeyed, ending up with my ass pretty much up in the air.

"Move your feet apart. And touch yourself."

Good lord. What was it about having this gorgeous man bark instructions at me that not only made my knees weak but also made me follow his instructions without question?

And while it wasn't really the time to analyze it, on the surface I knew. It was a relief to have someone else make your decisions, if only for a brief moment. It took away a level of responsibility and decision making that was a joy to have a break from.

It might not work for everyone, but it sure as hell worked for me.

I widened my stance and ran my fingers through my soaked lips. I looked back over my shoulder while Sammy sheathed himself with the condom.

"Face the window," he barked.

All righty then.

Next, his hands were on my hips, his cock bouncing against my ass.

"How're you feeling?" he growled.

I nodded, still facing the window. "Good, Sammy," was all I could muster.

Could anyone see us up here?

I guess that was sort of the point.

I wagged my ass in his direction. I wanted his cock. There was no hiding it.

"Are you ready for me, Bel? You want me to fuck you?"

I nodded, watching the ant-sized people on the street below. "Please," I whispered.

With his fingers parting my cheeks, he pressed into my pussy while I pushed back against him, impatient to satisfy my craving.

"Easy, baby. Easy," he said, rubbing his hand over my back and playing with small strands of my hair. "You know I love redheads, right?" he murmured.

Then, in one swift movement, he was all the way inside me. I shrieked from the shock and initial pressure of being stretched wide. But in spite of it, I bucked back against him.

It didn't matter how much it might hurt or how sore I'd be later. I wanted him to fuck me until I was dizzy from the pleasure.

And he did.

The heat we'd created in bed—eating, drinking, and

teasing—was nothing compared to what were doing now, searing every inch of me, inside and out.

He leaned forward, slipping his hands under my breasts and pulling my nipples. "You like it? You want more?" he murmured.

"Please. Yes, please, Sammy," I begged, loving his cock.

He pounded until I had to brace my hands against the window for purchase, hoping his thrusts wouldn't launch me right out of the hotel and into the air. I was close. So close…

And then I came like I never had, screaming, writhing, and grinding, trying to catch my breath. My throat was dry and hoarse and just when my legs began to quiver and got close to giving out, he gripped my hips so hard I knew I'd have marks later.

"Fuck, fuck, fuck, I'm coming," he hollered during his intense release.

I reached back and clutched one of his hands on my hip. "Sammy, I don't think I can stand any longer."

He gathered me up and got me to the bed just in time.

"HEY, KATE."

I lowered my voice since I was in the office. Not that anyone sat that close by, but I didn't want to advertise my personal calls, especially since my emails had been read.

It didn't matter that I was involved with the boss.

Correction. Boss*es*.

I still had a job to do and wasn't about to start slacking now.

Ever since I'd told Kate that my emails weren't private, she'd taken to calling me. "Bel, Len told me he saw you in a casino with another guy. Sweetie, you need to be careful. I'm worried for you."

That made two of us. The coffee I'd had for break-fast converted to churning acid, and just in case I got sick, I pulled my trashcan close.

So it *was* Len who I'd seen. Fucker. My eyes weren't playing tricks on me.

No matter how much I wished they were.

"Thank you, Kate. Thank you for letting me know."

"He kept asking me questions about you. But I told him I knew nothing. Because I actually do know nothing."

To protect Kate and myself, as the guys had suggested, I'd told her little about where I was or what I was doing, aside from giving her a phone number to reach me.

It would be better for everyone that way, they'd assured me.

And now I could see why.

"Bel, promise me you'll be careful."

Was she kidding? Of course I'd be careful.

But hopefully I'd not have to look over my shoulder for long. As soon as I shared this latest bit of news with the guys, they'd be all over 'taking care of it.'

Whatever that meant.

Len was doomed. The guys had no tolerance for people who fucked with them or the people they cared about. I was sure of that.

Which made me hesitate, briefly, about telling them.

Would it mean a death sentence for Len? And if so, did I really care?

Honestly, I did. Maybe I was an idiot, but he was such a pathetic loser. Did he deserve their wrath?

I was pretty sure I knew the answer to that.

27

DOMENICO "DOM" BONETTI

*A*FTER *WORK TONIGHT*, *return to the penthouse. There, you will find a new dress. Put it on and head downstairs, where a driver will pick you up.*

PS. We are going to a party.

I pressed *send*, and waited for Bel to come back to me with a litany of questions about where we were going and why, and anything else that would give her an excuse to come into my office.

Actually, if I were honest with myself, I wanted her to come to me with her questions, not so much because I liked questions—because I didn't—but because I'd barely seen her over the weekend and I'd been so goddamn busy at work all day I'd only seen her long enough to get my lunch.

I wasn't even able to eat with her, which put me in a shittier mood than I was already in.

But she had no questions. No visit to my office. Instead, I got one word.

Okay.

Well, that was easy.

When you own shit and have a lot of money, you get invited places. People want to be your friend. It didn't matter whether you were the biggest asshole in the world, people sucked up. I could have a sparkling personality and just ooze charisma, but without the hotel and all my assets, I'd never get invited to a goddamn place.

And success begat success. Our assets put us at the top of the Vegas social heap, and the social heap provided more opportunities to keep amassing more assets.

"Well, if it isn't Dominic Bonetti."

I turned to find the host of the evening's party, Charles Thidwick. Rumor had it, his was a fake name, to go along with his fake English accent, and his fake story that he'd just come over from 'across the pond.' But I didn't give a shit. He was a fun guy and as long as he didn't mess with me or any of my businesses, he could waltz around in a pink tutu for all I cared.

He'd ingratiated himself to the movers and shakers in Vegas—myself included—and his parties were an opportunity to see a lot of the people I needed to, all in one night.

"Charles," I said, taking his extended hand.

He sipped his scotch and scanned the room. "Think we're gonna have some good pussy tonight, my friend?"

Jesus. Aside from his carefully cultivated fake life, all he cared about was getting laid. It was pretty funny actually. When you were like Charles, you were a walking wallet to most women. He took them out and paid, and they put out. He felt it a fair exchange.

Not so sure about the women.

"I can't comment on that, Charles, but I do have a friend coming. In fact, I think that's her right now."

Bel passed through the revolving door like a glowing star. As she scanned the crowd, presumably looking for me, all heads turned in her direction.

The dress I'd chosen for her was nothing short of perfection. I raised my glass in her direction and when I caught her eye, she tilted her head, smiling, and made her way over.

If I'd had second thoughts about bringing her tonight, they'd all just vanished.

Her silky dress was low-cut, of course, because I'd chosen it, with two thin straps that passed over her shoulders and all the way down her back, where they joined with the rest of the dress at the small of her back. Because the front of the dress was on the skimpy side, and the back was nonexistent, she couldn't wear a bra.

Which had been my intention.

And as she made her way over to me, her perky tits jiggled the smallest amount under the green silk, rubbing her nipples just enough to make them stand erect.

"Fuck me, Dom. Is that your woman?" Charles gulped.

"What do you think?" I said, walking away to greet my lovely red head.

Her hair, gathered in a puffy confection at the nape of her neck, left curly tendrils floating around her face. Exactly how I liked it.

She grasped my fingers. "Dom," she breathed. "What a beautiful party."

I could barely take my eyes off her. But because I didn't want to be a weirdo creep, I forced myself to look around the room with her, checking out the movers and shakers of moneyed Las Vegas. It was an attractive and well-heeled crowd, one I'd easily been accepted into when I took over my dad's business and it was clear I was to inherit all his money, too.

Turning back to the lovely Bel, I brushed my fingers along her cheek, across her shoulder, and down her arm, leaving a wake of goosebumps on her pale skin. I didn't care that she was my employee. It didn't matter at the moment. Actually, it didn't matter, period. I'd known that since the first day she'd come to my office for her interview.

I knew I wouldn't be able to remain at the party for long. My urge to get home and get her naked would outweigh any important business associates I needed to say hello to.

"Well, this party *was* beautiful, baby. But when you arrived, it faded into the background."

She looked down at the clutch she held in both hands, a pink tinge spreading across her cheeks.

I loved a humble woman. My dick did too, and it stirred, reminding me of the fact.

"Thank you for the dress," she said, looking back at me. "I just love it. I don't think I've ever seen anything so gorgeous."

I didn't think *I'd* ever seen anything so gorgeous, myself.

I took a step back to take her in. "Why don't you turn for me? So I can see all of you?"

She dropped her hands at her side, and did a quick spin, yards of green silk swishing around her legs when she came to a stop.

"I knew you'd blow that dress out of the water. Goddamn, baby."

"Thank you, Dom. And not just for the dress."

God, what she did to me. Guileless, but proud. I liked that.

I took her hand. "Let me show you around."

As we pushed through the crowded room, I stopped every few feet to make my obligatory greetings and introduce Bel. Both the men and women had a hard time taking their eyes off her, so stunning was her green dress against her pale skin and fiery hair. She clung tightly to my fingers until Charles tapped me on the shoulder.

"Dom, my friend, could I steal you away for five minutes or so? I have a new business associate for you to meet."

I whipped around, fixing my face with an expression designed to tell Charles I did not appreciate being interrupted. But standing right behind him was one of the new Russian syndicates. The very man I suspected had been making trouble for Sammy, Tristan, and me.

What the fuck was he doing at Charles' party?

I sighed loudly. "Darling. Can you excuse me for a few minutes? The mezzanine is that way and there are sofas if you want to grab us a seat," I said, pointing to an area of the party that wasn't too crowded yet.

Charles liked to pack them in at his parties, I suspected to make himself look more popular than he was.

Bel looked from me to the men, immediately assessing the importance of my request. "Of course. I'll meet you there. After I get a fresh champagne."

She glided away through the crowd, her dress perfectly outlining the cheeks of her round ass.

"Dom, she is one hell of a beauty," Charles said, his

fake English accent slipping since he'd had a few drinks.

I barely paid attention as Charles attempted to get me to engage with his new Russian friend, distracted by counting the seconds to get back to Bel. As it was, I realized I'd been pulled aside more for Charles to show off that he knew me, than to discuss anything of significance. Which annoyed the shit out of me.

I reached for the phone in my pocket, pretending to have an important call.

"Excuse me, gentlemen," I said, putting the phone to my ear and taking the steps to the mezzanine two at a time.

It was hard to describe my need to set eyes on Bel again, except to say that when I did, it was like getting a cool drink of water when parched with thirst. That's what it was—a relief to confirm that she really did exist, and that she was mine.

I whipped by the bar for two fresh champagnes and joined her on the sofa, where she looked happy and relaxed.

"Sorry about that, darling. Charles doesn't always have the best timing."

She waved her hand. "No need to apologize. He wanted you to meet someone."

"True. But what he would have picked up on, if he had any common sense, was that spending time with you tonight is my priority. Not meeting his new Russian buddy."

She smiled and seemed like she wanted to say something. Finally, after a deep breath, she did. "Something… awkward just happened."

"What? Tell me."

That ex-boyfriend had better not be anywhere in the vicinity.

She laughed lightly and patted my leg. "Nothing horrible, believe me. But I went to the ladies' restroom and when I was in the stall, I overheard two women talking about me."

Oh shit. This could be a rough crowd, beyond the veneer of phony smiles.

"I take it they weren't talking about how pretty your dress was?"

She shook her head and laughed. "Not exactly. Their words were much less flattering than that, focusing on their opinions that you should be with someone more sophisticated, like them."

Christ. I was not surprised. At all. Annoyed, yes. But not surprised.

Bel seemed to take the insults in stride, but I was pissed she'd had to bear them at all.

"Do you know who they were?" I asked.

"Yeah." She pointed out the culprits.

Who happened to be the wives of two of my business associates.

I'd always known they were horrible bitches.

While I couldn't undo what had already happened, I could put the women on alert that if something like that happened again, their husbands' business dealings with me might come to an abrupt end.

In fact, I'd contact their husbands tomorrow and let them know exactly that.

I ran a finger along Bel's neck, over her gold choker, and down the deep V of her dress. "I'll take care of it, baby. I'm sorry that happened. But I'm sure I don't have to tell you there are a lot of assholes in this world."

She nodded in agreement. "Seriously. It's incredible how many assholes there are. I've known a few myself. Actually, probably more than a person should in a lifetime."

We clinked our glasses.

Another reason I wanted to take Bel in. She hadn't been given a fair shake.

But she was getting one now.

28

DOMENICO "DOM" BONETTI

THE RIDE HOME, while only ten minutes, was the slowest fucking ten minutes of my life. We kissed in the back seat of my limo the entire ride, and just before arriving at the hotel to head up to the penthouse, I reached under her dress to find her pussy soaking wet.

She gasped when I touched her there. I wasn't surprised. I knew she'd be responsive. After all, I'd listened to Sammy fuck her just a few days before and if the entire hotel didn't hear them, *that* would have been surprising.

I'd had to jerk off twice just to be able to leave the goddamn house.

When we got inside the penthouse, Bel headed

215

straight for my room. But I caught her hand and led her toward her own.

"You don't like your room?" she asked.

"I like it a lot. But it's just mine. The other guys are the same. Your room is for… getting together."

We didn't have many rules, but keeping our apartments to ourselves was one we stuck with. Not that it would be the worst thing in the world to get Bel naked on my bed, but it was more exciting to use her room for all things carnal.

I kissed her forehead. "Go to your room, undress, and wait for me." I turned and headed to the liquor cabinet.

There was a brief hesitation and her high heels clicked across the floor, getting quieter as she reached her room.

I poured a scotch for myself and a champagne for Bel. I thought back to the women who felt so free to trash her when they thought she couldn't hear. It amazed me how some people thought they were better than others, especially for no reason other than they'd managed to marry rich husbands, which didn't take any skill aside from being beautiful and willing to suck cock. The minute those trophy wives lost their good looks, their husbands would be on to their next flavor of the month, perhaps promoting their behind-the-scenes mistresses to the role of third or fourth wives.

Yeah, their husbands would be hearing from me, and those bitches would learn a lesson the hard way.

But I had better things to think about right now.

I entered Bel's room and quietly closed the door. I lowered the lights and set our drinks down.

"You know how fucking beautiful you are?" I asked, striding toward her.

She sat with her hands in her lap, completely naked, waiting on the edge of her bed. When I stood in front of her, she craned her neck to look up at me.

"Thank you," she whispered.

I took her chin between my thumb and forefinger and just shook my head. Her crazy red curls, which she'd unpinned in the limo, fell around her face and over her shoulders, partly covering her breasts. She looked like a goddamn Lady Godiva. She was so perfect I almost didn't want to touch her.

Almost.

Gripping her chin, I pulled her to her feet, and without her heels, she came only to my chest. I turned her to face away and toward the bed.

With my hand on the back of her neck, I directed her until she was bent in two, balancing with her hands on the bed. I smoothed my hand over the pale flesh of her ass.

"Brace yourself, baby," I said.

She stiffened, unsure of what was coming next.

I smacked her ass so hard she yelped and fell forward on the bed.

I pulled her back to her feet and took a seat on the edge of the bed, pulling her to my lap.

She looked at me, attempting something like defiance, but her glistening eyes gave her away.

Was she about to cry? I wouldn't blame her. A good ass smacking worked wonders for releasing pent-up emotions.

But when I pressed my mouth to hers, she melted into me, any previous tension leaving, the way it did when you stepped into a warm bath.

"Have you been spanked before?"

She shook her head no.

"Did you like it?"

She looked away and shrugged.

I turned her face toward mine. "I can't hear you."

"A little," she said in a small voice.

"I can't hear you."

She tensed, just like I wanted her to. "*Yes.*"

I sat her on the bed and stood in front of her again. "Take out my cock."

She smiled, possibly because she was back on her game, and opened my fly while I shook my jacket off and tossed it to the floor. Reaching through a tangle of shirttails and boxers, she gripped my hard on.

I almost came right there in her hand, but I wanted to make our first time last. It would be one she'd never forget.

"Suck me."

Dropping to her knees, she took me in her mouth. The sensation of her tongue on my cock exploded from my balls to my spine, and without thinking about it, I thrust my hips forward until I hit the back of her throat.

She gagged briefly, but then relaxed, saliva dripping down her chin, mascara running from her watering eyes.

"God baby, that feels nice."

She took a deep breath through her nose, and with her hands on my ass, pulled me even deeper than when I'd shoved myself in her mouth.

I wasn't going to last long.

If it were any other woman, I'd just let myself come in her mouth. But with Bel, I had to be inside her. There were no two ways about it.

"Stop," I murmured.

She either didn't hear me, or ignored me, the suction on my cock becoming stronger.

"I need you to stop," I said, a little more loudly.

Okay, she was definitely ignoring me now.

So I gently pulled out of her greedy mouth.

Reaching into my pants' pocket, I retrieved a condom. Since she'd only opened my fly, my belt was holding my pants up, leaving me still, for the most part, dressed. I released my buckle, and everything fell to my ankles.

I sat on the edge of the bed, whipped off my shirt, and sheathed myself.

"I'd like to fuck you now."

One corner of her mouth turned up. "I'd like that."

"Good. C'mon," I said, patting my thighs.

She straddled me, holding my shoulders.

I parted her glistening lips to make way for my cock, slipping inside her until she gasped.

"You okay, baby?"

"Yeah," she said, watching my cock slide in and out.

I pulled her onto me with one swift effort, impaling her until she screeched. Her head fell back and her hair flew as I pushed and pulled her on my dick.

I fucked her like I'd wanted to since the first time she'd come to my office with her eyes full of hope. I was happy to give her something no one else would.

And I didn't just mean my dick.

29

ANNABEL "BEL" SIMMONS

I MUST HAVE FORGOTTEN to close the blinds before I went to bed, because the blinding sun was scorching my room. A sunny room was lovely until the temperature got tropical.

But, given that I was in the best hotel in Vegas, and in a custom-outfitted penthouse built exclusively for the owners, my bedroom's AC came on with a soft hum before I could even think about adjusting it.

Regardless, I was awake now, and falling back to sleep was unlikely. I turned to see if Dom were still there, and to my surprise, he was.

I would have thought my master of the universe

would rise at the crack of dawn to manhandle some sort of business deal. Or someone who'd crossed his 'syndicate.'

Since I'd heard mention of the guys buying and selling guns, I'd not learned much else that would offer clues as to how they spent their days, aside from what I saw as they managed the hotel and casino, and pawn shops. It seemed strange to straddle such a spectrum of the business world—from the best hotel in Vegas, to tacky pawn shops in the worst parts of town. And then there were the quasi-legal—or just plain illegal —activities.

The contrast was dizzying.

But also a turn-on.

I'd never known predictable men and I didn't see any reason to seek them out now. These guys were exciting. I never knew what they'd come at me with next.

Like Dom's smacking my ass the night before.

Without making a sound, I turned over to face him as he slept naked, half under and half on top of the covers with his face buried in a pillow. He looked so innocent. Sweet, almost. His body rising and falling with his breath, hair sticking up in several directions.

I was dying to touch his smooth skin, to run my hand down his back and over the mounds of muscle that made his hard ass, but I didn't want the moment to end. In his sleep, he was mine. All mine. I didn't have to share him with anybody or anything else in the world, not even his own thoughts.

With only a slight movement, I propped up my pillows to read while Dom snoozed next to me, and when I reached for the book on my nightstand, I knocked over the champagne he'd given me the night before. It crashed and spilled everywhere.

I'd never even had a sip of it.

And of course, my clumsiness woke him.

He looked up from his pillow with a start, like someone who didn't remember where they'd fallen asleep.

"Sorry. I wanted to let you sleep."

He ran his fingers through his bed head. "It's okay. Good morning."

Pulling the covers over us, he turned on his side, propping himself up on his elbow with his head in his hand.

Looked like he might stick around for a while.

"How'd you sleep?" he asked, running a finger along the side of my bare breast.

My nipple immediately engaged, turning hard and pointy, and leaving me shivering. "Very well, thanks."

I'd lost track of how many times he'd fucked me, but I was pretty sure that if there were such a world record, we'd be up there with the champs.

"Hey, Dom, I wanted to tell you something."

"What's that?" he asked, twirling a strand of my hair around his finger.

"I've… I've been with the other guys. Sammy and Tristan."

He looked up at me with that blank face of his. He must be one hell of a poker player, never giving anything away.

With his face, that was.

"I know. It's fine."

Well, then. No reaction was a good reaction, right?

"I know you guys do that thing where you date the same woman. Or something like that. But I just wanted to be really honest that you weren't the first. I was with Sammy the other night and Tristan before him."

He smiled and nodded. "I know. They told me. We talk about these things."

A rush of heat blasted my face, and I buried myself in the pillow to hide it.

"It's nothing to be embarrassed about, baby," he said, stroking my shoulder. "It's normal for us. It will become normal for you too."

My head popped off the pillow and I looked at him, not sure what to make of his words.

The word 'normal' sure was getting a workout lately.

"If you want it, that is," he added.

I whipsawed between feeling like I was cheating on someone, and feeling safe and desired.

It was as good a time as any to ask my questions. "Have you done this before?"

Ugh. Was I going to regret asking this?

But it didn't matter. I had to know.

"We have. And it's been great. Once you're in a relationship like this, Bel, you won't want to go back to a traditional one. It will feel so… lacking."

I wasn't as sold on it as he was. But I was trying to keep an open mind.

"What about it do you like?" I asked.

Again, I held my breath.

"Well, for starters, I like to watch and be watched. These guys are my best friends, so it's freaking awesome to share something like a woman. And it's also erotic as hell, keeping our girl on her toes, wondering what lies around the next corner."

I liked that answer. It made things a little clearer. Not completely, but a little.

"Do you like to be watched?" he asked, brushing the back of his hand over my nipple.

"I… I don't know. It sounds… I don't know."

What I wasn't telling him was that our conversation was making me hot. Like *if he didn't fuck me, I'd have to finish myself off*, hot.

He pushed the covers down and jumped out of bed, his erect cock bouncing up and down. "I'm going to get Tristan and Sammy."

"I… I don't know…" I stammered.

"Say no and I won't. But I think you want this. And I think you'll like it."

He looked at me, waiting to say that I wanted him—and the guys—to usher me into their world of sensuality.

Shit, I'd never been with two guys, let alone three.

"Do it," I said quietly. "Go and get them."

I pulled the covers up and lay there, frozen in place, afraid they were going to find I wasn't worthy of their affections. If I weren't so paralyzed, I might have run to the bathroom to fix my hair and brush my teeth.

Instead I couldn't move.

I didn't understand it. Why did they want *me*? They could have any woman they wanted, I was sure of it. There was no shortage of women interested in them, as evidenced by the way the female employees of BCL Enterprises stopped by Dom's office several times a day with the most basic of questions.

Not that I was jealous or anything.

Maybe this was one of those questions I'd never get an answer to, because some things in life were not meant to make sense. They just *were*.

Footsteps approached my door. I wasn't sure what was louder, them or my pounding heart.

Why did Dom have to run and get the other guys? What was he trying to prove? Or was it a test, to see if I could handle all of them?

Calm down. Calm the fuck down.

I even took a deep breath.

Just when I thought I might faint, which I didn't know was possible lying down like I was, my bedroom door sprang open and Sammy stuck his head in. "I understand I've been summoned?"

Something about his quiet voice and smiling eyes smoothed the edges of my anxiety. I was still nervous, but his face reminded me the guys were on my side. This was no adversarial relationship. We were a team. I was just the newest member.

Emboldened, I pushed the sheets down to give him an eyeful. There was no sense in being shy now. I wanted to give myself to him and the others.

Sammy growled quietly and moved toward the bed. "That's what I'm talking about, baby."

He pulled his T-shirt over his head, and dropped his jeans to the floor.

"Hey now, don't get started without me."

I looked behind Sammy to find Tristan entering my room with Dom right behind.

Holy shit. They were all here at once.

"Isn't she gorgeous, guys?" Tristan said, tossing aside his polo shirt and pants. "Especially wearing our choker."

"I'm the only one she hasn't fucked yet," Tristan said, as if I weren't in the room right in front of him.

Sammy slapped him on the back. "Well then, I guess it's your turn, brother. If she'll have you. But if she says no, I won't blame her. She knows to save herself for the best." He put his hands on his hips and puffed out his chest, laughing.

Next thing I knew, I was surrounded by three gorgeous—and naked—men.

"Come over here," Sammy said, reaching for my hand and directing me to the middle of the bed.

If it hadn't dawned on me before, I now realized why the room had such a gigantic bed. I lay in the middle of it, reaching my arms overhead, where Dom caught my hands and held them in place.

Tristan, on my other side, slowly parted my knees, spreading my most private parts open for his inspection.

"Wow. What a pretty pussy. Shaved, and so pink." He ran a finger up my slit and brought it to his mouth. "And fucking wet."

With his hands under my thighs, he pulled me toward him until he could taste me, licking me from top to bottom.

"God, that feels so nice," I breathed, arching into him while Dom held my arms.

"I can think of something else that feels nice," Sammy said, moving toward me, erection in hand.

I was writhing under Tristan when Sammy rubbed his cock on my face. It was warm on my cheek, leaving a thin snail trail of precum. With my hands pinned, I couldn't stroke him, so I turned my head and opened my mouth, ready to suck him if he would let me.

And he did.

Between my legs, Tristan probed me with one and

then two fingers. When they were deep inside, he pumped with the same rhythm he was licking me.

With the two guys working me, Dom held my hands in one of his, and out of the corner of my eye I saw him start to stroke himself.

Plain and simple, I was in heaven.

I was making three gorgeous men feel good, and they were doing the same for me. Floating in a sea of erotic sensation, I hoped it would never end.

I heard a condom wrapper open, and knew Tristan was sheathing himself. While Sammy continued fucking my mouth and Dom stroked himself, Tristan hoisted my hips up, putting my legs over his shoulders.

"Are you ready?"

All I could do was grunt.

So he impaled me with his hard cock.

Even with my mouth full of Sammy, I still managed to scream as Tristan filled me to my limit. Behind me, Dom's breath quickened, and I heard his strokes get faster.

There was no doubt at least a couple of us were about to come.

With a tortured groan, Sammy plunged into my mouth one more time, flooding me with hot cum. I took as much as I could and the rest dribbled from of my mouth, where it ran into my hair and the bed below.

At the same moment, Dom released my hands and

hovered his cock over my breasts, covering them in cum, just like my mouth and face.

Released by the two guys, I gripped Tristan's arms for purchase, and let him pound my pussy until my mind went blank. One orgasm, followed by another, rolled over me until I couldn't see or hear, or even say anything besides a few grunts and groans. All I could do was feel, and the only thought running through my mind was *don't stop, don't stop, don't stop.*

30

SAMUELE "SAMMY" CAPUTO

GODDAMN, had Bel turned out to be sexy as fuck.

Her reaction to our touch was explosive. By the time the three of us were done with her, she was nearly catatonic.

Hot. As. Shit.

Dom had chosen well. He'd recognized something special in her the first time she'd walked into his office. His immediate offer of a job ensured she'd stick around, at least for as long as she wanted. He hadn't even interviewed anybody else. Why waste time? He'd scored masterfully on behalf of us all.

I'd thank him if I didn't think he was already bigheaded enough.

While I replayed the sexy session of the night before, I steered my car in the direction of the shitty part of town. I didn't mean to sound like an elitist asshole—god knew I'd grown up on the wrong side of the tracks. But now that I'd gotten a bit of success under my belt, I realized just how shitty the shitty areas of Vegas were. Heading back over there reminded me of where I'd come from—something I could live without. Although, I supposed it kept me humble.

Yeah, right.

These sojourns to Vegas's less *cheerful* neighborhoods seemed to be how all my Mondays started lately. I never got to roll in anymore around nine-thirty or ten and look over the weekend's restaurant reports while sipping my expensive, imported coffee.

Yeah, I was *that* kind of asshole.

This morning, I was meeting Dom and Tristan at some Russian creep's place to let him and his loser team know if they didn't stop fucking with our guns, they'd be headed back to the motherland in pine coffins.

Maybe we should have just taken care of them from the get-go, warnings be damned. But Dom was trying to run our business differently from how his old man had, and that included attempting to collaborate with folks who, in the past, would have been abject enemies.

That wasn't to say the Russians wouldn't eventually *become* abject enemies. But we were giving them the chance to work with us first.

A kinder, gentler sort of syndicate was how I looked at it.

Like the way we'd given our friend Joe, with his under-the-radar poker games, the opportunity to hold one more game before he paid us back. As promised, he'd shown up the next day with full payment. His card room was off to a good start and we got paid back. Win-win for everyone, and no blood was shed.

I backed my car into a parking space in case I needed to get out fast and nodded at Dom, who'd parked on the other side of the lot. I spotted Tristan's car on the street, finishing our little triangle of observation.

At the agreed-upon time, the three of us exited our vehicles and headed for the secured front door of the dumpy office building the Russians ran their operations out of.

The intercom buzzed. "Yes," a flat, Slavic-sounding voice called.

"BCL Enterprises here," Dom said evenly.

The door buzzed with an unsettling screech, and we passed through to a small anteroom that smelled of cigarettes and animal piss.

They let us cool our heels for a few minutes because that's what guys did when they were trying to establish a hierarchy. I could understand their wanting to put us in our place. They were on the bottom of the rung of Vegas organized crime, and trying to get some sort of footing. Unfortunately, they thought there were shortcuts, and that by fucking with us they'd accomplish some sort of intimidation. Maybe move up a couple rungs.

That might work in Russia, but it didn't work in Vegas, and it sure as hell didn't work with us. In fact, the longer they dicked with us, the harder we'd have to come down on them, something they wouldn't like and something I'd rather not have to bother with. When tempers flared, who the fuck knew what could happen.

After a couple minutes, Tristan started pacing. It was not a good sign. We'd pegged him as the 'sensitive one' of our trio ages ago, but the downside of that was his wicked temper when pushed too far. The man had high highs and low lows, and I'd seen them all, as well as the moderate times that fell in between.

I knew him well enough to know he was gearing up for a fight.

What a way to start a Monday.

Especially since we'd had such a fucking incredible connection with Bel over the weekend.

As much as I didn't relish confrontation with other local syndicates, I knew they came with the territory. Since they were a part of the job, I didn't spend a lot of time thinking about them. But something about that morning's meeting was leaving me unsettled.

If I were honest with myself, it was because of Bel.

My feelings for her aside, we had a responsibility to her. And the kind of risks we took on behalf of our syndicate business seemed a little riskier—and a little less responsible—that morning than they had in the past.

I found myself wishing we'd sent an intermediary to deal with these guys, rather than risking our own necks. It might not have been as impactful as us showing up here, but it would have been a hell of a lot safer.

And the longer these fuckers made us wait, the less safe our rendezvous became.

I looked over at Dom, who was checking his gun. Yeah, it had turned into *that* sort of morning, and Tristan and I followed suit. As soon as I'd tucked mine in the back of my jeans, the door to the lobby blew open and we were faced with a huge bald guy in a velour track suit and shiny white sneakers.

Par for the course.

"Come," he growled.

A single glance from Dom let me know we'd follow our usual protocol by spreading out in whatever room this guy led us to. That way we could watch what was going on from all angles, and it made us a more challenging target, should it come down to that.

"Well, if it isn't BCL Enterprises, as you call yourself," a heavily accented guy said from behind a grotesquely oversized, gilt desk.

"Hello," Dom said, making no move to shake hands.

And so it went, two factions, one after a larger slice

of the pie and the other defending the slice it already had. If I'd seen it once, I'd seen it a hundred times.

Tristan and I let Dom handle the conversation.

"You need to stop interfering with our business," Dom said.

The Russian raised a bejeweled finger to his face and scratched at the corner of his mouth.

These guys were so fucking predictable.

"I don't know what you are talking about," he said with a smirk.

Dom sighed loudly. "You're saying you had nothing to do with holding up our last shipment? Even though our men saw you there? In fact, I think your very face was recorded by our security cameras."

The Russian belted out loud laughter. "What is it with you Americans? You have cameras everywhere. Did you also see me take a piss? Because if you really want, I can show you my big dick right now."

He started to get to his feet, but Dom drew his gun. The room froze with tension as Tristan and I, and the Russian goons, put our hands on our weapons.

The Russian sank back to his seat. "We grow our business by any means possible. If that doesn't work for you, too fucking bad."

Big mistake.

The Russian had just sealed his death warrant.

You don't say shit like that and expect to live a long life.

"Sorry to hear that," Dom said, shaking his head

sadly. "You're leaving us with no choice but to take action."

What a way to start the week.

And it was more unfortunate than ever because I kept seeing Bel's face.

Just as I pictured her porcelain skin and fiery hair, the first shot rang out. I swung around and knocked the gun out of the hand of the guy closest to me while Tristan smacked another in the head with his own weapon.

As the guy behind the desk, now with a bullet between his eyes, slumped over, Dom turned to the other men in the room, now disarmed. They sheepishly raised their hands.

One of them cleared his throat. "Mr. Bonetti sir, maybe you give us job now?" he asked in his broken English.

So much for loyalty.

Tristan scooped up their weapons as we headed for the door.

Dom, turned to them. "We'll let you know."

And we left.

"Fuck, Dom, that was a close one," I said as soon as we were outside.

"It's always a close one, Sammy," he barked, and climbed into his car.

We all hit the road, heading in different directions. It was how we operated.

I SECURED MY WEAPONS IN THE SAFE IN MY OFFICE AND took the stairs down to Dom's floor. I was dying to see Bel after the morning's clash. Something about her was so… reassuring.

Just before I rounded the corner to her desk, I stopped to eavesdrop on her phone conversation.

"Hey, Mags, did you get the tuition money I sent?" she asked.

Who was she sending money to? Wait, she had a sister, right?

She sighed happily. "You're welcome. I'm happy to help. You are so close to finishing, Sis. It's amazing."

She laughed. "Oh, Mags, you won't have to put me through school, and you don't owe me a darn thing. I have a good job now and am glad I can help you."

It all added up. She was paying for her sister's school. Why hadn't I realized that before? It was exactly the sort of thing Bel would do.

I was more impressed with her than ever.

Not so much with myself for listening to a personal conversation.

Just then, Dom's door blew open.

"Gotta go," she said quickly, dropping the phone into her desk drawer.

I was tickled she thought she had to hide her phone calls. Did she think we'd fire her or something?

I strolled around the corner just as Dom reached Bel's desk.

Thank god he'd beaten me there because I was speechless.

Bel was more stunning than usual, wearing a slim black dress, her hair gathered into a messy braid that hung forward over her shoulder. She wore barely any makeup save for dark red lipstick that accented her shapely lips.

"Hi, guys," she said, popping to her feet.

Dom looked my way. "Sam, did you need something?"

Shit. I was busted.

"Um, yeah, I was coming down to… talk to you for a moment."

He nodded. "Cool. Just give me a sec."

He returned to Bel, discussing a list of people she was to call. She studiously took notes.

I loved that while she was part of our lives, she still took her work seriously. She could probably get away with slacking if she wanted to.

But she wouldn't.

I was also happy to see her fill out a bit. She was still barely what I'd call a curvy woman, but her willowy figure was softer now, thanks to all our eating out. And damn, did it look good on her.

"Sammy? Hey, Sammy," Dom said, snapping his fingers in front of my non-responsive face.

"Oh, sorry. Hey, my phone just buzzed. I'll come

back to see you later." I hustled for the stairs to return to my office.

Damn it. I'd wanted a minute alone with her but it would have to wait until later. I had an offer for her and I wanted to see her face when I presented it.

Soon enough, asshole, soon enough.

31

ANNABEL "BEL" SIMMONS

"You can't be serious, Sammy."

He looked at me with an expression that said, *yes, I am fucking serious.*

I jumped up and down a little in the elevator as we sped to the ground floor. And just for good measure, before the doors opened, I gave him a nice, juicy kiss on the lips. The corner of his mouth turned up in a smile, and I knew I'd made my handsome, rock 'n roll guy a little happier that afternoon.

Or a lot. Sammy was certainly easier to read than the stone-faced Dom, but even then I sometimes couldn't tell what was going on in his mind. I'd catch him from time to time staring at me, just watching without saying a word. At first, I suspected he thought I was unattractive or otherwise lacking. God knew I couldn't hold a candle to the other women in the office, with their on-trend clothing, smooth hair, and perfectly Botoxed faces. But I'd made peace with my wild curly frizz a long time ago, even if it was more odd than chic. I was still not much of a fashion girl, preferring jeans and sneakers, but I'd watched the other women in the office and had learned how to put a nice outfit together.

Not that the guys seemed to care how I dressed. They liked me for *me*.

It really was unfathomable, and every now and then the question of *why me* bubbled to the top of my thoughts. But I pushed it away just as quickly in the knowledge that it didn't really matter. The guys, whether impossible to read like Dom, or wearing his heart on his sleeve like Tristan, had proved they had some level of fondness for me and wanted me to stick around.

Would they have moved me into their penthouse if I were just the flavor of the week?

I knew they'd done this with other women in the past. Not that they'd given me any details. But I'd gone through the desk and dresser drawers of my room and found some photos that the last woman staying there had apparently forgotten to take with her.

They were snaps of a beautiful brunette, about my height and weight, with the guys in every photo.

I'd wondered for a moment if she'd left them on purpose. As a message to the next woman.

Remember, you're only temporary like I was.

As wonderful as the guys were, those imagined words haunted me. But I kept my eye on the prize. I was helping my sister, getting work experience, and even saving some money.

And college might be an option, as Maggie had promised. If I wanted to get a degree at some point, I knew she'd make good on her offer to put me through.

Where would the guys fit in all this? I had no idea. But I didn't know where I fit into their lives, either, at least beyond the short term. Shit, they might tell me next week that they were done with me.

Had they done that with the beautiful brunette?

Had she worked for them too? Perhaps she was the lucky former PA who'd retired to the Caribbean.

The elevator doors sprang open when we reached the lobby, and Sammy stepped aside so I could pass through first. I'd never known men with manners like his, and while they seemed old-fashioned, I was learning they were a sign of respect.

I was also learning that real men *showed* respect. They didn't, like Len and the other guys back home, feel like they were giving up their manhood by acting like gentlemen.

Sammy took a couple of my fingers in a spontaneous clasp and the usual shiver shot through me, causing my breath to catch. Fortunately, the casino was blaring loud enough to drown out all but the loudest voices. He never heard a thing.

We burst through the two-way doors leading to one of the hotel's restaurants, the one where we'd had dinner at the 'chef's table' not long before.

Sammy waved over the chef. The chef who ran the top restaurant in the top hotel in Vegas.

They did the guy handshake thing where they half-shook, half-hugged.

"Nice to see you again, Bel," he said, giving me a normal handshake. "Sammy tells me you're interested in cooking. I'd be happy to set up a *stage* for you sometime."

"*Stage*?"

He laughed. "A *stage* is the French word for an internship in a chef's kitchen. You get to try a little of everything and see if you like it. It's unpaid, which is the only bummer."

Holy crap. Who knew such a cool gig existed. It would be amazing... if you didn't have to work for a living.

"That sounds really cool but my days are full working for Sammy and the guys. Could I do a *stage* on the weekend?"

I felt so fancy throwing around a French word.

"Sure. Weekends are crazy busy and we always need the help. If you think you could hang."

For a moment I thought he was mocking me, but his eyes were kind and sincere.

When we got back to the casino floor, I turned to Sammy. "Oh my god, thank you. It would be so cool to see how a professional kitchen works."

He took a step closer, so close his lips were nearly touching my forehead. "We want to give you all the opportunities you deserve. Now, if you'll excuse me, we guys have one more meeting and then we're done for the day."

My heart sank when I realized Sammy wasn't free to hang out. But it was all good. I hadn't had much time to myself lately, and it would be nice to have an evening alone. And I knew exactly what I was craving.

I got back to the penthouse and threw on my uniform of choice—jeans and sneakers. It wasn't that I didn't appreciate the beautiful clothes the guys had gotten for me, but to be honest, if they'd never given me a single gift I would have been perfectly content.

Did the brunette from the photos feel the same way? Or did she relish the gifts they'd showered on her?

I straightened my choker and stuffed my hair into the ball cap I'd gotten at one of the hotel gift stores, put some money in my front pocket, and headed out.

I was going to treat myself to a nice burger and a beer at a diner I'd seen a few blocks away. It would be good to get a walk in and see some of what made the Las Vegas Strip so famous. I'd be quick and return before the guys got home. They'd never know.

32

ANNABEL "BEL" SIMMONS

Excited about my little excursion, I wove around the tourists crowding the sidewalks in awe of flashing lights and exploding fountains, who were taking photos and discussing the shows they wanted to attend —and where they could win the most money at slots.

Just as I passed a father trying to comfort a kid whose ice cream had tumbled off its cone, there was a tap on my shoulder.

Darn. One of the guys had spotted me and was going to be pissed I'd ventured out alone.

But it wasn't one of the guys.

Unfortunately.

It was the scruffy, backwards-baseball-cap-wearing Len.

My heart thudded against my chest and blood roared through my ears.

The street's flashing lights even blurred a little. It was like everything around me slowed. There was less air to breathe.

It couldn't be. God no. And while I didn't want to believe my rotten luck in being found, I was almost relieved that the inevitable had finally happened. The suspense had been agonizing, and now the waiting was over. He'd said he'd come for me, and he did. I'd never doubted him.

His hair jutted from under the edges of his cap like he was overdue for a haircut. Dark circles under his eyes made him look old and unhealthy.

I felt for the cell phone in my pocket but was too frozen to think of who I might call.

The guys? My sister? Kate at the motel?

It didn't matter. None of them could help me now.

All the goodness that was new in my life, allowing me to help my sister and create a better future? It was like the universe had just seized it out of my clawing fingers and told me *that's not for you honey, sorry.*

Who the hell was I trying to kid.

Len's fingers tightened around my wrist, and he smiled. It was his smile that had first captivated me back in West Virginia, the one that had told me he was different from all the other guys there.

And it was the smile he wore when he'd last thrown a hard object in my direction.

Joke was on me.

"How are things, *Bel*?" he spat.

In the middle of the sidewalk where we stood, the crowd maneuvered around us like we were nothing more than an annoying rock in the middle of a fast-moving stream. Just a momentary bother. Don't mind us.

My hand flew to my gold choker as if it had some sort of magic power that would alert the guys to my distress.

Which wasn't a half-bad idea.

But that's all it was—an idea.

And I'd made the mistake of drawing Len's attention to it.

"What the fuck is that thing? A dog collar?"

He scowled and looked at it more closely.

While I was being feted with fancy clothes, a penthouse apartment, and so much food I was starting to put on weight, Len was closing in on me. I'd known he wouldn't go away easily and in spite of Kate's warning, I'd foolishly hoped he couldn't get to me.

And yet here I was, back in his clutches.

Len pulled me away from the pedestrians I was hoping might discern that I needed help, and sat me down on a curb, his hand tightening on my wrist.

"I need to talk to you, Bel. I'm sorry to have to force

you like this, but I didn't know how else to get your attention since you ran out on me."

Sitting low on the curb, I stared straight down at my sneakers with my knees pulled up, scrunching myself into as small a ball as I could.

"Bel, please listen. I'm sober now. I'm clean. And I've started winning again."

I looked at his pleading face, knowing he was full of shit.

But he wasn't giving up. "Look, I've moved to a better room at the motel. One with a kitchen. It's real nice. You'll like it."

My stomach roiled at his assumption that I'd be seeing his new motel room.

"Bel, I'm sorry. Sorry for everything. We've been through so much, you can't just throw it away. Please give me another chance. You won't regret it."

"Len, no. I can't. I would never get back with you—"

Before I could finish, he'd yanked me to my feet. "Look, Bel. You'll never get rid of me. I'll always find you. And I'll always drag you back to where you belong. I saw you walking in that casino, all dressed up like you're somebody fancy. But you know what? You're just a girl from West Virginia, who ain't nothing special. So stop acting high and mighty. You're no better than me, or anybody else."

Is that what I seemed to him? High and mighty?

And what if he were telling the truth, that he'd never let me alone? Would I go through the rest of my life looking over my shoulder, waiting for him to walk up behind me on some crowded sidewalk, where he could so easily drag me right back to the life I'd tried to get away from?

And what about the guys, anyway? I was probably risking my life, working for men involved in some of the things they were. Was being with them really that much of an improvement, when they could throw me out anytime they wanted, like they might have done to the brunette in the photos?

Len might not have much of a future, but he wanted to be with me for the duration.

Surely that was worth something, wasn't it?

Christ, was I losing my mind?

I needed to buy some time. Figure out what I needed to do.

"Okay. Okay. Can I just go back to the pent—I mean, my room, and pick up my things?"

He frowned over my stumble, still highly suspicious I might bail on him again at any moment.

"Yeah. Let's go. I'll come with you."

Shit. I couldn't let him see the penthouse. Or the guys.

"Okay. Let's go."

We made our way back to the hotel. I was desperate for a way to keep him in the lobby while I went upstairs.

And the guys. What would I say to the guys, aside from thanking them for all they'd done for me?

They'd understand. It was simple. Len would never let me go. It was pointless to think otherwise. And I was just a plaything for the guys anyway.

At least with Len I knew I had something long term and stable. And maybe the guys would let me keep my job. It might not be easy to get another one with my police record.

Anyway, they'd wanted to 'share' me. What the fuck did that mean?

I wouldn't have to worry about it anymore.

"Wait here," I said to Len when the elevator doors opened.

"The hell I will," he said, reaching to keep them open.

"Len, do this one thing for me. I will be right back down. I don't want… anyone to see us together. It would not be good for you."

Awareness lit up his face. "All right. I'll give you fifteen minutes, no more. And if you try to pull anything funny, you know I'll find you again. You'll never get away from me, Bel."

The penthouse was dead quiet, thank god. I scurried to my room before anyone got home and sat down on the edge of my bed, waiting for the tears. But they didn't come. I was too numb. So I started packing my stuff and composing in my head what I'd put down in a note to the guys.

33

TRISTANO "TRISTAN" LASTRA

"Hey, Bel. Going somewhere?"

Startled, she looked up from the pile of clothes strewn across her bed, and an empty suitcase in the middle of it all.

Her eyes were bloodshot and her face blotchy, and she looked at me like she'd been caught doing something she shouldn't have.

She avoided my gaze. "Um, yeah. I am going somewhere."

She grabbed a pile of neatly folded T-shirts and jeans, and stuffed them in her suitcase.

"Must be pretty casual, wherever you're going."

"Yup." She started stuffing the suitcase faster.

What was going on?

I looked to see if she still wore the gold choker we guys had given her, and there it was, shiny against the delicate skin of her neck. Not that she could remove it without one of us, anyway. We were the only keyholders.

"Can you stop for a moment, Bel, and talk to me?"

Sighing, she finally looked my way. Her face was covered in sadness, and if I wasn't mistaken, she looked tired—not tired from lack of sleep exactly, but more weary. Beaten down.

It was the same way she'd looked when she first came to us.

"Sweetie. What's going on?"

"I'm going back to Len."

Because she'd said it so matter-of-factly, it took a moment to register.

Then it sunk in. "Len? Your ex-boyfriend Len?"

She nodded and crossed to the bathroom, returning with an armful of toiletries, which she stuffed into a backpack.

"Were you going to tell us about this? Or were you just going to disappear?"

She looked at me blankly.

I guess she was better at hiding her feelings than I was. Actually, I was shit at hiding my feelings. Always had been.

She put a hand on my arm. "Don't be sad."

"I'm not. I'm not sad. You need to do what you need to do."

It was true. I wasn't sad. I was actually devastated. I just didn't want her to know. If she really wanted to go back to Len, she was free to do that. But I'd rather she was leaving us because, I don't know, maybe she'd gotten a great new job in another state, or had met a guy—any guy—who was not the dirtbag Len.

But to be left for that creep? Jesus, had we been that far off about her? Had our efforts to help her really been that meaningless?

"Look, Tristan, Len is clean and sober now, and is finally making some money at poker. He is in it for the long term. Unlike you guys."

Fuck. Had someone just kicked me in the gut? Because it sure felt like it.

She pulled the zipper closed around her suitcase. Dragging it off the bed, she wheeled it toward the door.

I wanted to stop her. To block the door and not let her pass or at least grab her arm to force her to stay put. But I knew what agency meant, and if anyone deserved theirs, it was Bel.

"I'm not sure what to say. I didn't see this coming. I don't think any of us did."

She pulled her hair forward over one shoulder and hoisted her backpack on the other. "If it makes you feel any better, neither did I." Her voice was flat and dull, just like the look in her eyes.

But when her voice cracked, I knew she felt something. She could deny it all she wanted, but her voice betrayed her.

"Bel," I called after her. "You don't have to do this. Please. Think about it. Have a talk with us before you do anything. We'll change things if needed."

Her lips quivered, but she tried to press them together into a thin smile anyway. "My note is on the coffee table."

The penthouse door opened, then slammed shut. In the distance I heard the elevator ding.

What the fuck just happened?

"You didn't try to stop her? Tris, tell me you tried to stop her. You cannot be that… stupid."

I glared at Dom, which I thought was pretty generous because what he really deserved was a belt across the mouth. But he was upset. We all were.

Sammy just sat quietly, reading Bel's note for a second and a third time—like if he read it once more, he might find something he'd missed, and that something would be that she wasn't leaving.

I sighed. "If we held her here, we'd be no better than the loser boyfriend."

Dom got in my face, the lines around his mouth tight and drawn. "I'm not saying we *force* her to stay. We *convince* her to. *Persuade* her to. Or have you forgotten all your negotiating skills?"

He was so goddamn frustrating, so in control that when something didn't go his way, he lost it.

I raised my voice. It couldn't be helped. "I'm telling you, Dom, her mind was made up. He bullied and intimidated her. She didn't see any way out but to go with him. She was as fucking determined as anyone I'd ever seen."

He turned away in an attempt to hide his slumping shoulders. Was he finally getting that no amount of arm-twisting would have made a difference?

But that didn't mean there wouldn't be another chance.

Only, what if there weren't? I'd never had the chance to tell her I loved her.

That's right. I loved her. And now she might never know.

I thought we were giving her everything she needed. But the one thing she wanted—something permanent—we'd never even talked about.

I laughed out loud and the other guys frowned in my direction. I didn't care. I was an idiot. How could I have not known that's what she wanted?

She wanted a commitment. And I'd completely missed that.

To be fair, so had Dom and Sammy.

So I guess we were all idiots.

34

ANNABEL "BEL" SIMMONS

"OH MY GOD, honey. Good to see you!"

Kate clapped her hands together and ran around the motel lobby desk to throw her arms around me.

It felt good. It really did.

She put her hands on either side of my face. "I've missed you. I mean, I know you have something good going on, but I still miss you."

The smile dropped from her face as she spotted the suitcase and backpack behind me. Frowning, she gave me her wicked side-eye. "What's this? I thought you were just coming by to say hi. Why do you have a suitcase, Bel?" she asked, her voice getting higher with each word.

She was surprised. Tristan was surprised. Dom and Sammy would be surprised, if they already weren't.

Hell, I was surprised.

The only person who wasn't was Len. He'd assumed all along he'd eventually get what he wanted.

And he'd been right.

"Kate, I'm back. Len brought me back. He just ran across the street to the liquor store."

She wrinkled her nose. "Huh?"

I looked at the threadbare carpet to avoid looking at her. "Len caught up with me. Told me he's made some improvements. That he's clean and sober and winning again."

Her head snapped back. "No. No, Bel, none of that is true."

I appreciated her concern, but how the hell could she know what Len had been up to? And did it matter? He'd always find me. The misery of wondering when he might show up was a worse fate than actually being with him. At least I knew what to expect, even if it wasn't much.

It was more than I'd had with the guys back at the hotel. I'd never know when my last day with them was until it came.

"It's okay, Kate," I said with a small, hopeless laugh. "It almost doesn't matter. I can't go through life wondering when Len might show so I might as well... succumb. You know, get it over with."

Succumb. Such a repulsive word. And yet...

"Oh, Bel…" she said, her eyes filling with tears.

I grabbed my backpack and wheeled my bag toward the door. "Thanks, Kate."

It was all I could think to say. I had no good excuse to offer, only my thanks for her care.

I was sweaty and out of breath by the time I'd gotten my bags up the stairs to the third floor—the elevator was out of order, as it always was.

Len might have bragged that he'd scored a better room now that he had some money, but all I could see from the top of the stairs was a better view of the cheap motel across the street, a mostly boarded-up strip mall, and a mini-mart with one car in the parking lot.

A far cry from the penthouse.

I let myself in with the key Len had given me, and entered my new home.

Moments later, he joined me, carrying a bag holding multiple bottles of liquor. He looked out the door before he closed it, as if he were watching for someone. "Hey, any of those pussy guys you working for follow you here?"

Pussy guys. I'd love to hear him say that to their faces. It would be hilarious. Painful for him, but hilarious for me.

"No, Len."

I looked around his new room. He was right, it was larger and had a little kitchenette, but that was about all it had going for itself. And larger meant more room for more mess. Every surface was littered.

Kate was right. The fucker had lied to me.

There were beer bottles everywhere.

"Len, you told me you weren't drinking—"

"Bel, don't start. Just don't start with your bullshit. It was the only way I could get you back here with me, where you belong. You think your place is over at that fancy hotel working for those rich fuckers?" He moved closer until he was right in my face. "Well, it's not. You belong *here*. With *me*."

He slammed a beer bottle down so hard it broke right in his hand. He looked at it and laughed.

"Now, come to daddy," he said, beckoning me with a finger.

There'd been a time when I couldn't wait to be with Len. I thought he knew what he was doing because he'd known more than the other guys I'd been with. But now that I'd spent time in bed with Dom, Sammy, and Tristan, I had a different perspective on sex.

"I'm not in the mood right now, Len. Maybe later."

I bent to unzip my suitcase.

But before I could finish, he grabbed my shoulder and pulled me toward him.

I put my hands on his chest. "Stop it, Len. I'm serious."

He pressed me up against the wall. "Oh, baby's *serious*. Well, fine. I have all the time in the world. And get rid of that stupid gold thing around your neck."

Shit. I'd totally forgotten about the choker. There must be some way to get it off without the actual key. Like maybe with a screwdriver. But I'd worry about that later.

Len plopped down on the bed and put his hands behind his head. Within moments, he was snoring.

Thank god.

I took the opportunity to go back downstairs.

"Oh my god, Kate. You were right."

She ran around the counter toward me. "Are you okay? He hasn't hurt you, has he?"

"No. I'm fine. I guess I shouldn't be surprised. He wasn't going to suddenly clean up his life and make a fortune gambling."

I was fucked.

"Bel, you have to call the guys from the hotel right now. They'll come over and help you. Don't be crazy. You know what I'd give to have guys like that taking care of me? I'd be out of this shitty place so fast."

I shook my head. "I can't go back. They'll think I'm a total loser."

Actually, they probably already thought I was a total loser.

"Plus, Len will find me again. He'll always find me."

Unless the guys could *really* take care of him…

"You're insane," Kate said, shaking her head. "Please think about it."

I took my time returning to the room. As much as I wanted to go back to the guys, I just couldn't.

And Len was about to let me know why.

"Where the hell were you?" he barked when the click of the door woke him.

I sat on the edge of the bed, resigned. "When you fell asleep, I went downstairs to talk to Kate."

He narrowed his eyes at me. "Don't try and leave me again, Bel. You'll be sorry. You will."

His words sent shivers down my spine.

I reached for my handbag, one of the few things from the guys that I'd taken with me, but Len snatched it out of my reach.

"Before you go getting any ideas, I already grabbed your phone." He tossed my cell up in the air, catching it like it was a toy. "I always wanted a nice phone."

My heart sank as I climbed into bed next to Len, fully clothed, and laid awake all night.

35

DOMENICO "DOM" BONETTI

"YOU GUYS HEARD ANYTHING?"

I stopped my pacing long enough to see Sammy and Tristan arrive in my office.

"No, Dom. Not a thing. You?"

I shook my head.

Fucking women.

I didn't get it. I just didn't get it. We'd given her everything. Absolutely everything. And she still bailed.

I'd hoped that even though Bel had gone back to her loser boyfriend, she'd still show up to work. Kind of a stupid wish, no doubt, but it was something to hang on to.

Instead, the morning came and went and there was no sign of her.

Nor was she answering her phone.

Our sources had let us know that Len had been lurking on the strip, hoping to find Bel. But we knew he wouldn't be able to get to her, because we'd stressed numerous times she shouldn't go out by herself. And she hadn't.

Until last night.

I didn't know what the hell had come over her.

After the other guys had gone to bed the previous night, I'd gone into Bel's room. I wanted to touch her things, to smell her. See if she'd left behind anything of herself aside from what we had given her.

But all I could find were the clothes and shoes that she apparently didn't want—or more accurately, didn't need—in her new life with Len.

I hadn't expressed how I felt about her. Maybe that was a mistake. It wasn't my style to share much, and that had worked against me in the past. You'd think I'd learn my lesson.

Apparently not.

One of the reasons she took off was that she believed we couldn't offer her any sort of stability or long-term commitment.

Shit, I hadn't even known she was looking for something like that. But she was in a vulnerable position, and I could understand. While things were moving fast between us, she'd not known us long. Why should she trust that we'd always be there for her?

I lay down on Bel's bed. There were a few strands of red hair on her pillow, and I picked them up to twirl in my fingers.

I was half-tempted to save them but that would be creepy stalker-dude shit. I threw them back on the bed, and got the hell out. If she felt the need to leave us, I wasn't going to belly ache about it.

Except that's exactly what I did, all night long.

I'd lain awake for hours before finally picking up a book that kept me occupied until the sun came up. For some dumbass reason I got to the office early, thinking there was a sliver of a chance that she'd show. But why would she? She wanted out.

"We have to find her," Sammy said. "You guys haven't met this Len dude. He's a no-good mother-fucker. I couldn't live with myself knowing she's with him because she feels like she has no other option."

Tristan nodded slowly, pushing my office door closed. "Maybe that's the issue. We didn't show her that she did have choices."

"But Tris, you made the point that we can't coerce her."

He thought for a moment. "Right. Exactly. She made a choice, but that's because she thought that was the only choice she had."

Sammy raked his fingers through his hair. I

suspected he'd not gotten much sleep himself, as evidenced by the bags under his eyes. "I say we head over to the motel. She's friends with the woman who manages the front desk. She may be able to help."

"ARE YOU THE GUYS WHO BEL... WORKS FOR?"

"We are. Have you seen her?" I asked.

She sighed grimly. "Yeah. She's upstairs. With him."

Sammy stepped up to the counter. "You might remember me. I took her out of here last time."

She nodded. "I remember."

"I know you're not supposed to do this, but can you tell us what room she's in? We have to get her away from that creep."

A big smile crept across her face, and she laughed. "I can do whatever the fuck I want. They're in room three-twenty. In fact, I'll do you one better."

She bent behind the counter and returned with a card key. "Here's the key to their room. Have at it. Go get our girl."

Sammy accepted the key and bowed his head. "We really appreciate this. Thank you."

When we got to the room, I knocked softly but there was no answer. I knocked harder and still nothing.

I looked at Sammy. "Try the key."

He inserted it and the door clicked. Pushing it open slowly, he let me pass through, then Tristan, then himself.

First thing I saw was the boyfriend sprawled on the bed passed out, snoring loudly, probably having tied one on.

Bel's things were scattered about the room, but there was no sign of her.

She'd clearly been there. But where had she gone?

"You guys cover him," I said, gesturing to the sleeping boyfriend. "Bel?" I called quietly. "Bel, are you here? It's us."

I heard some hangers clang together in the closet and inched my way over there, stepping over empty beer bottles and cigarette butts. When I reached the closet, I drew my weapon and checked the guys. They were ready to restrain Len when he woke up.

I reached for the door and yanked it open. "Put your hands up," I screamed.

"Please don't hurt me," a quiet voice said.

I looked into the dark closet and found Bel, cowering in a corner.

"Holy shit," I said, dropping to my knees. "Are you okay?" I looked over her face and arms for any obvious injuries.

"Hey. What the fuck is going on here?" Len said as he tried to sit up.

But Tristan pushed him back down. "Shut up, loser."

He tried to sit up again. "Get out of my room, you fuckers." Then he saw Dom helping Bel to her feet. "Get off my girl. I'll kill you. I swear I will."

Sammy cracked him across the face with his gun.

Bringing his hands to his face, Len screamed in pain as blood poured from between his fingers.

"No, no," Bel mumbled.

"Are you okay? Are you hurt? I asked.

She looked down. "I'm okay. But how can you stand to look at me? I'm… a disgusting loser. No better than him, over there on the bed."

I took her by the shoulders. "Bel, you're nothing like him. We're going to make sure he never bothers you again. You don't have to be with us, but you don't have to be with him, either. You have choices. And the decision is yours."

Her pretty face crumpled and she began to sob.

"C'mon sweetie," I said, putting an arm around her shoulder. "Let's get out of here."

She slumped against me and as we walked down the corridor, I heard Sammy and Tristan giving Len a good going-over. We were taking him to the bus station later and treating him to a one-way ticket out of town.

And we'd make it very clear that should he show up again, it would be the last thing he ever did.

Tristan got behind the wheel when they were done, and as soon as we were on our way back across town, Sammy turned around from the front seat.

"Bel, I'm so sorry you didn't know what you mean to us. It was a mistake to hold that back from you."

She looked up from where she'd snuggled into Dom's chest. "What do you mean?"

"We want you to stay with us. All of us. For the long term. Our moving you into the penthouse might have started as a sexy game, but we've all… fallen for you."

"I second that," Tristan said from behind the wheel.

She looked up at me. "What about you, Dom?"

I smoothed the hair back from her forehead and nodded. "Yeah. I do."

"Bel, we can live wherever we want—in the hotel, or in a huge house somewhere. Whatever you want," Sammy added.

The brightness I'd found so charming began to seep back into her eyes and she straightened up in her seat.

"How did I get so lucky?" she sighed.

I was going to say the same about us guys.

EPILOGUE

Len was gone. Kate confirmed he'd left the hotel, and my sister Maggie confirmed he'd been seen at home around town a week or so later, acting like he was a big Las Vegas poker player. But people were asking—if he were so successful, why was he back in West Virginia instead of raking in the bucks in Vegas?

Some people are just too stupid to even tell a good lie.

Turned out he had to leave Vegas for more than one reason. He owed someone the money they'd fronted him for poker and of course he had no way to pay it back. The people who ran the poker games were some of the meanest in town, I'd heard. So Dom, Sammy, and Tristan had done him a favor by showing him the door. He would have ended up a dead man, otherwise.

I'd started my weekend stage at the restaurant. It was hard, demanding work and it wasn't glamorous, but then I wasn't a glam girl, anyway. I had all the gorgeous clothes the guys had gotten me, but happily wore jeans and sneakers in the kitchen. The chef, who'd initially seemed so nice, yelled at everyone, including me. But I loved it.

It was just the way chefs were, everyone told me.

I kept my weekday job working for BCL Enterprises. I wanted to be with Dom, Sammy, and Tristan as much as possible. They'd helped me to see I deserved better, and I'd finally gotten to the place where I knew that was true. I don't know what took me so long to figure it out. Sometimes we are our own worst enemies.

We think our external enemies are bad, but it's the internal ones that will really do a job on a girl.

Not only had I been able to send enough money to Maggie that she could quit all her crappy little jobs and take more classes to finish college faster, but I was also helping out Kate. Dom had gotten her into the casino training program where she could work her way up the ladder in any number of jobs in the gaming industry.

Oh, and those nasty bitches who'd talked smack about me in the ladies' room that night? Well, they'd invited me to join their club. I was going to tell them hell no, but then I thought I might spend some time with them and show them how nice people behaved.

Not bad for a girl from West Virginia with a police record.

And the guys seemed pretty happy with their variety of businesses. The hotel and its restaurant were winning awards, the pawn shops were no longer being robbed, and nothing was getting in the way of whatever it was they did with guns.

I didn't know any more than that, nor did I care to.

The guys said I was their good luck charm.

Actually, I think it was more like they were mine.

Did you like *Her Dirty Mafia?*
Check out the next book in the
Men at Work series:
Her Dirty Mountain Men

I hope you loved reading this book as much as I loved writing it. Please visit my store to learn more about my books, and to buy directly from me!
https://mikalaneshop.com/

ABOUT THE AUTHOR

Dear Reader:

I'm USA TODAY bestselling romance author Mika Lane, and am OBSESSED with bringing you sassy, steamy stories with imperfect heroines and the bad-a*s dudes they bring to their knees. I'll always bring you my signature humor and heat, topped off with a modern-day happily ever after.

My first book ever was *The Day I Ate the Milkyway*, a true fourth-grade masterpiece illustrated with crayons and bound with construction paper and glue. Nowadays, steamy romance gives purpose to my days and nights as I create worlds and characters that tickle the imagination. I live in magical Northern California with my own handsome alpha dude, sometimes known as Mr. Mika Lane, and two devilish cats named Chuck and Murray.

A dual citizen of the United States and Ireland, I have on more than one occasion spent my last dollar on a plane ticket somewhere, and am always planning my next escape. I often try new recipes on unsuspecting friends, search out hiding places to read undisturbed, and sadly kill every houseplant I bring home.

I LOVE to hear from readers when I'm not dreaming up naughty tales to share. Visit my online shop https://mikalaneshop.com/ and say hello https://mikalaneshop.com/pages/meet-mika.

xoxo, Mika